6-WEEK ROTATION

AUTHORIZED BY AUGMENTED HUMANS RECORD ACT OF 1965, EXECUTIVE ORDER AUG-001, NIXON PROTOCOLS (1972)

ON THE BACKBURNER

SOLEMN JUDGMENT

BOOK 1

A 6-WEEK ROTATION NOVEL

2023 Convention Exclusive Edition

DEREK M. KOCH

Special Thanks:

There are so many folks who stood behind me, whether they realize it or not, that helped to make this Convention Exclusive edition of *On the Backburner (Solemn Judgment Book 1)* a reality. In no particular order, thank you to Chris, Dominique, Jeff, Joe, Matt, Mike, Tom D., Tom G., Tracey, Steve, and David. Also, thank you to my old high school Creative Writing teacher Mr. Bill Roberts whose lessons and mentorship I still rely on to this day even though it's been over thirty years since I last sat in his classroom at Cheyenne Central High School. Additionally, I've shared a gaming table with so many superhero role-playing game groups over the years, and I owe every one of those players a marvelous thank you as well. And finally, I lied. I did have a particular order in mind for this Special Thanks page. I saved the best for last. Thank you, Beth, for believing in me, letting me ramble on and on and on about this novel for months on end, and for constantly supporting me no matter what.

Cover design by Joseph Schultz and Derek M. Koch.

6-Week Rotation logos design by Alistair Hughes. Visit Alistair on line at Shoreline Creative (https://shorelinecreative.co.nz).

PROLOGUE

Abigail Andrews allowed herself a brief moment to close her eyes and inhale deeply. The smell of drying leaves and the bite of the cool autumn air nibbled at her nostrils. She wanted to hold on to those sensations for just a second or two. The Pacific Northwest – when it wasn't raining – was her favorite place to be during her favorite season, and she hoped that her grandfather was wrong about there being trouble in downtown Portland. She just wanted to enjoy a peaceful Fall day.

The downside to it being a peaceful Fall Day in downtown Portland was the number of other people out enjoying their own peaceful Fall days, especially where her grandfather indicated she and her partner Hence Williams needed to be. Blackstone Hall, the five-story PSU student residence building with the sculptured Egyptian pharaoh sculptures on either side of its front door, stood across the street from them. The two from-the-torso-up half-statues stared blankly back at them. She'd have to ask Hence about them later, but now wasn't the time.

Now was a time to worry about the number of students and staff, teachers and pedestrians in downtown Portland's Park Blocks. Specifically, the number of potential witnesses and even more potential victims concerned her.

"Abby?"

She felt her teammate nudge her. Hence Williams stood beside her, trying to get her attention, but she wouldn't call him Hence. Not in the field.

"We're working. It's Pentacle." She cast a steady stare at him and made sure to use his codename to further make her point. "Revenant."

He smiled back at her. "I know. You just seemed . . . distracted."

"I'm just trying to enjoy the moment before whatever Grandfather said is going to happen happens."

Revenant nodded. "I understand."

Pentacle looked around. She and her Solemn Judgment teammate didn't stand out. It was downtown Portland, and no one paid much attention to the two of them standing in front of the library across from Blackstone Hall. She wore a burgundy long line camel hair coat over her costume, and even though it hung open across her front, no one seemed to mark her as anything other than a red-haired young woman who might have even been a PSU student.

Hence Williams – Revenant – also was dressed as nondescript as he could muster, but his clothing choice was limited to what he was wearing in the 1920s when he was trapped in that collapsing Egyptian tomb he tried to plunder. He was stuck wearing what he had on when he somehow found his way back into the world. No one would have guessed he was missing part of his humanity and maybe part of his soul thanks to whatever he encountered beneath the sands of ancient Egypt. No one paid any mind to what looked like a middle-aged man wearing dusty cotton trousers and a buttoned-up Norfolk jacket. Fortunately, he hadn't manifested his khopesh sword yet, so he didn't attract any unneeded attention.

The black man walking toward them, though, did draw attention, and Abigail knew he did so on purpose. Even from a block away, she recognized Troy Norris – Voodoo Cowboy – striding toward them. His long black sleeveless duster flapped behind him, his exposed-to-the-Fall-chill arms practically flexing as made his way to the members of Solemn Judgment. He wasn't part of the team, but he was a Portland local, and his area of expertise often times meant he and her team worked . . . how did her grandfather put it? They didn't work together.

They worked concurrently.

Voodoo Cowboy raised his hand and called out to them. "Pentacle! Revenant!"

She rolled her eyes. They were trying to keep a lower profile.

At least he used their codenames.

She glanced over at Revenant who returned Voodoo Cowboy's wave with a quick gesture of his own. Revenant looked back to her and shrugged. "I called him."

"You know Grandfather doesn't approve."

"There's two of us here, Abby." He caught himself. "Sorry. Pentacle. And Deacon made it sound like this could get messy."

She sighed. "Fine." Hence was right. Her grandfather did say he was tracking something big. "But if he asks, you're telling my grandfather that it was your idea."

Voodoo Cowboy closed with them and was able to join the conversation. "Your grandfather doesn't approve of me or what I do."

Pentacle shook her head. "It's your . . . methods."

Voodoo Cowboy flashed a bright white toothy grin and tipped his Gambler cowboy hat. "Sure. Let's call it that." He brazenly flicked his wrists. His hands glowed, and red energy outlined his fingers as he made quick fists. He let his hands slowly open, and the glowing energy expanded and coalesced into what looked like Old West guns. He'd told Pentacle before they were modeled on Colt Navy revolvers, based on what Wild Bill Hickok used, but that didn't matter right now.

Instead, what mattered was three people stood across from one of the residential buildings at Portland State University, and one of them just drew a pair of glowing guns.

Revenant made it worse when he closed his eyes, concentrated, and a semi-transparent khopesh sword slowly appeared in one of his hands.

"Subtle, guys." Pentacle pulled her coat closed. She loved the season, but it was chilly.

And when Blackstone Hall exploded in front of the three superheroes, she wasn't chilly anymore.

CHAPTER 1

Thirty-two minutes before the explosion . . .

Arturo Banks let himself in through the front doors of Blackstone Hall. He had a backpack full of books from the library next door slung over his shoulder, his laptop in a messenger bag, and a foot long from the sandwich shop down the street in his hand. Art had a long day of studying ahead of him, but he didn't mind. He missed practice and being part of the football team, but he enjoyed his studies almost as much, so he couldn't complain.

At least, he couldn't complain about the coursework. He could complain about the aches in his right leg from all the hardware that had to be put in to rebuild his thigh and knee after the accident on the football field last year. This was his first Fall after the disastrous football practice that ended his career and scholarship, and even though his physical therapist told him he should expect to feel the changing colder weather in his leg, he didn't like it.

He could complain, but he also knew it wouldn't do any good. His mother wanted him to come back home after his accident, but despite growing up and living in Carthage his entire life before starting college, he wasn't ready to leave Portland to return to Texas. Not until he finished what he started, with or without a football scholarship.

He wouldn't complain to his mother, and his father only wanted to talk about his classes and his plans for after graduation. Football was simply no longer something they could discuss.

"Hey, Arto! Wait up!"

Art instinctively held his leg out to keep the door from closing behind him, and tried to hide his pained grimace when his classmate and friend Peter Middlemiss jogged up to the entranceway.

"Thanks." Peter grabbed the door and followed Art. "Aren't you supposed to be in class?"

"Big project coming up. I need to get a jump on it, and my advisors got me the afternoon off. What about you?"

Art paused before heading down the hallway toward his room when Peter didn't respond right away. "Peter?"

Peter wasn't paying attention. He was watching the door they just entered, and dropped his backpack.

Art shifted his own backpack. "Hey. What's going on?"

Peter shook his head and blinked his eyes. "Nothing. I just . . . do you hear that?"

Art shook his head.

"I thought I heard something." Peter started to reach for his backpack, but slowed and looked back to face Art. "Seriously. You don't hear that. It's . . . "

Peter's eyes corkscrewed back into his skull just before he screamed.

Art dropped his lunch and bags. He ran and caught Peter. Lowering him to the floor, he strained his ears, but couldn't hear anything out of the ordinary.

"It's so . . . loud. It's like a song."

Peter's face was losing its color save for the two bright spots of red that appeared at his temples.

Art felt his bad knee pop as he knelt on the floor cradling Peter. He looked around. "Somebody! Anybody! Help!" He looked back down to Peter and realized those two red dots at his temples weren't just color.

They were blood. Small wounds opened on either side of Peter's head.

Art fought the temptation to drop his friend on the floor and run. Instead, he cradled his head and tried to hold him upright. "Peter!" He glanced up again. "Somebody help us!"

The doors to the left and right leading down the opposite sides of the residential hall remained closed.

"It's like . . . music . . . like . . . " Peter's voice trailed off.

Art touched one of Peter's temples and tried to stop the blood. "Come on, man. Stay with me." At some point, Art had stopped kneeling on the floor. He was now sitting in the middle of the lobby, pressing his palms against Peter's temples.

He looked up at the front door leading outside. "Anybody! Please!"

He heard the main hall doors open behind him. He twisted his neck, and a rubber pain shot down his back and hips. Peter's head slipped from his grasp, and it bounced with a disturbingly hollow sound on the tile floor.

5

A woman with dark, disheveled hair and even darker eyes stood in the doorway. She wore a light blue windbreaker with messy smears of red across its pockets and waist. Her jeans were also smeared with blood.

Art tried to stand, but the pain in his hip made his legs and knees sloppy. The best he could do was push himself back toward the front door.

Two men filed out from either side of the woman and lunged at Art. He tried to kick away, but they reached him quickly and grabbed him by his arms.

"Pick him up."

Art tried to push back, but the two men – one with dirty blond hair and one with no hair at all – held him. There was strength in their hands, strength he wouldn't have expected.

He also hadn't expected to see wounds similar to Peter's at their temples either.

The woman approached, slowly, with solid purpose. "And who are you?" She reached for Art's head.

He tried to pull his face back, but she grabbed his chin. Art opened his mouth and started to scream.

The woman tightened her grip. "Don't. Shhhhh." She leaned closer and lowered her voice. "Wait, I can tell you who you are." She concentrated on his eyes for a moment before dropping her grip on his jaw. "Well, that's not entirely true. I can tell you who you were."

Art tried to shake free, but his captors held him still.

When the woman turned her back on him, he looked past her and saw others, men and women, all students, all with holes in either side of their heads, walking toward her. Their gait was uneven, but their eyes never wavered from looking at her, whoever she was.

She turned back on him. "Arthur . . . no . . . Arturo Banks. Arturo 'Take It to the Bank' Banks. Small town football star from . . . Texas, right?"

Art opened his mouth again to speak, to yell, to scream, but the woman made a cutting motion with her hand and the bald man clamped a hand over his mouth.

She continued. "Texas. And you came here on a football scholarship." She approached him again.

The woman kicked him in the right knee. Art's eyes bulged and he tried to slip a yell through the bald man's fingers. He was unable to hold his own weight, and slumped. The two men kept him from completely crumpling to the floor. The woman stepped closer to him. She smelled like dead flowers.

"You failed, Arturo. You got hurt. You lost your knee, your scholarship." She stood. "Your purpose." She looked at the broken college student pityingly, and then to her two followers. "Get him on his knees. I want to do this the old-fashioned way."

As Art was forced to kneel, he watched the woman reach into her pockets. When she pulled out her hands, each held a gleaming scalpel.

Art opened his mouth as wide as he could, let the fingers of the man holding him slip between his lips, and bit down.

The man jerked his hand free. Art did his best to spin around and bolt for the door, but his right leg refused to work the way it did before his accident. He managed to stay upright, but he didn't make it far.

"If you weren't broken, Arturo, that might have worked."

The blond and the bald grabbed him again. He could hear the woman getting closer. "Put him on his knees." The two men followed her command. Art tried to resist, but when one of them – he wasn't sure which one – kicked at the back of his leg, he went to the floor.

"It is fortunate for you that we met. None of this will matter. Your failing body. Your failing strength. Your failing purpose . . . none of that will matter."

He felt her breath on the back of his neck and she whispered to him. "You will be born again. You will be born again to me." She withdrew slightly, but he could tell she was still just behind him. Art felt two points of cold pressure on either side of his forehead, and he knew she held her scalpels to his temples.

He felt the metal blades push against his skin. "How do you know me?" He tried to understand while pushing his head forward to escape the blades.

She didn't answer him. "Hold him." The two men tightened their grip. The thin skin at Art's temples dipped, and then popped as the scalpel blades cut into him.

Art could barely make out the what sounded like dogs singing under the sound of his own screams.

The scalpels pressed into the sides of his head. He squeezed his eyes and tried to jerk away, but the metal just cut deeper the more he moved. He felt the pressure of the metal, he heard the singing hounds . . . and then the scalpels stopped plunging into him.

"Stillborn! We found it!"

At the sound of this new voice, the scalpels were withdrawn, first the left one, and then the right. At some point, he stopped screaming, but that absurd singing continued. His eardrums vibrated against the sound, and he didn't want to open his eyes. Cool blood trickled down the sides of his face. He felt his strength leaving his body, and slumped forward. The blond and the bald kept him from sliding completely to the ground.

The woman – was Stillborn her name? – stomped away from him. That much Art could hear, but as hard as he tried, as hard as he strained, he couldn't hear any of the conversation over that baleful singing. There were no words to the song, just barking and howling sounds that seemed to hit certain beats in time with his own thrumming heartbeat.

He did hear the woman come back to him, and as soon as she spoke, that strange singing stopped.

"Drop him."

Art couldn't imagine her sounding cooler than before, but yet, she did.

"And turn him over."

Art didn't fight the efforts of the two men as they rolled him onto his back. He finally let his eyes slide open, and realized he had been placed next to Peter's now-still body.

The woman stepped into his view. "We will continue this later, Arturo. You're not born again. Not yet. But I have other business here in this building to tend to. Here." She reached down and touched him with the tip of one of her scalpels. It felt like ice as she gently tapped his forehead. "Stay. Do not move. Do not run. Do not scream. Just stay. Your rebirth will continue soon."

She stood and addressed the others. "Leave him. He's going nowhere."

Art watched, frozen on the floor, as she and the blond and the bald left his view. He heard the three of them make their way deeper into Blackstone Hall, but whatever she said to the others, he could not make it out.

He closed his eyes and took a deep breath before trying to stand, but discovered the scalpel-wielding woman was right. He couldn't move. Art's legs refused to do anything other than barely twitch. Panic flooded his body as memories of his final football game threatened to overtake him. He mentally pushed back at those memories, that particular moment when what would have been a routine tackle ended his college football career and scholarship. In that one moment, the trajectory of his life changed. Everything he planned, everything he dreamed, all the sacrifices Art made to get to that one point in his life all took on a different meaning when he was hit from behind by a fellow player.

He couldn't stand then, and he couldn't stand now. Peter was no help. Art's fellow Blackstone resident lay in a broken and bleeding heap near him, unmoving and unblinking.

The woman and her people were still talking, and they were getting louder. With a shove, Art finally found the strength to force his head around, smearing blood on the lobby floor. They weren't approaching. Their voices were getting louder because they were . . . yelling? Screaming? When the woman – Stillborn – shouted, Art's ears ached, but he still couldn't make out what anyone was saying.

He tilted his head back toward the front door. Would any other students be coming to the Blackstone? It was mid-afternoon, and most everyone was in class, but there was a chance.

But he couldn't wait. He needed to lift himself from the floor the way he finally pushed himself off the football field. Like that game night, his legs still had feeling. He could feel them, and he knew if he could feel them, he might be able to move them.

Instead of the turf of the football field, cool tile pressed against his cheek. Fluorescent lights instead of stadium lights flickered overhead. And no one was chanting his name.

But he could still feel his legs.

Art slid his arms and hands underneath himself and pushed. Fiery pain raced down his hip and into his right thigh and knee. He clenched his jaw and ground his teeth against the lava-hot agony erupting at the base of his spine. After a quick inhale, he shoved himself from the floor.

He couldn't tell if he or Blackstone Hall itself was spinning. Art lurched, and yanked himself to the side to keep from slamming face first into the wall. That painful jolt stopped the spinning, but now his vision blurred. He took another intentional breath, this one slower and deeper. The wall felt safe, and he let his back lean against it.

After several more deep breaths, Art finally felt stable. He gingerly touched the left side of his head. His fingers touched the wound at his temple. He winced and jerked his hand back, but then touched the right side of his head. The scalpels had cut him, but the wounds didn't seem too deep. The bleeding would probably have stopped by now if he hadn't been struggling so hard to get to his feet.

He steadied himself, and tried to move forward. He took that step away from the wall slowly, but almost lost his balance when a sound startled him. Someone down the hallway – the same hallway the blond and the bald and that Stillborn woman took – screamed.

Art slapped his palms against the wall to keep from collapsing against it. He tried to focus. Who else was in Blackstone right now? He only moved in recently and hadn't made a lot of friends here yet. Most of his free time was spent on his schoolwork. His social circle shrunk significantly when he left the football team.

Whoever it was screamed again, and this time, it was cut short.

Art took another deep breath, steadied himself, and stumbled down the hall.

With every step, especially every step with his right leg, the floor felt soft and liquid-like. He used his hands to steady himself. At some point it occurred to him to use his phone to call for help, but by the time that thought fought its way to his mind, Art had already limped nearly to the end of the hallway and discovered his phone must have slipped out of his pocket back in the lobby. He briefly considered going back for it, but that was at least 60 feet ago. His leg might not make it back again. He chose to keep going forward.

At the end of the hall was one of the main doors. Beyond it was the perpendicular hallway that led to either side of the building and the individual dorms. A turn to the left, a few feet, then another left turn, and Art could be in his room. The thought of laying down right now, stretching his leg with no pressure weighing on it would be –

His thoughts cut short when he pulled the door open and instead of finding the connecting hall he spotted a hole in the floor.

Tile and flooring were torn away. A pickaxe lay to the side, but most of the digging and excavating was jagged and sharp, as if someone tore through the floor with their bloody hands.

Or several pairs of hands. Art leaned forward. The opening in the floor revealed another level beneath the building. Blackstone Hall didn't have a basement or lower level, but here it was.

And there they were. Two men – Art recognized one as a fellow resident – stood at the bottom of the opening. They were looking away, down what Art imagined to be another hall or room, and, more importantly, not back up at him.

Art's right knee twitched and a jolt of pain shot from his leg through his hip to his shoulder. His strength left him, and if not for his twisting at the last moment, he would have fallen down to that lower level. Small chunks of concrete and a shard of some other stone material skidded beneath his feet and tumbled below onto the two students. By the time Art recovered and was able to lean forward again, the two students were looking back up at him.

"Uh . . . guys?" Art could see from here that they both had open wounds on both sides of their heads. Blood trickled from their temples to their collars. One of them – Art thought he remembered his name was Todd – just stood still, head cocked up, staring blankly at him. The other – Art could not remember this one's name – reached up, and then over to the edge of the opening between them.

Art followed Not-Todd's outstretched hands with his eyes, and that's when he saw the rope ladder pounded into the main floor of the building.

He tried to step back, but his hip lit up with another rush of pain. Art squinted against it, and he did not fall. But he also did not move, and Not-Todd was climbing up the ladder. Art felt his surroundings sway again so he went to steady himself. The student crawled to his feet in front of Art, grabbed him by the shoulders, spun him toward the opening, and pushed him.

Art reached frantically for the edge of the ragged hole in the floor, but his fingers only touched the pickaxe. His hand wrapped around its handle, but it just slid with him as he slipped beneath Blackstone Hall's main floor.

He felt all sensations of pain leave his body, and only briefly realized it was because he no longer had his own weight working against him. Gravity took him, and took all the pressure off his joints and legs.

And then he hit the floor beneath. He landed on his chest, and the air rushed out of him like toothpaste stomped from a tube.

CHAPTER 2

Seventeen minutes before the explosion . . .

The jolting pain of landing face left Art stunned, but it was quickly overshadowed by the cascading explosions in his hip when Todd yanked him to his feet. Art tried to focus on something other than the pain. His eyes landed on Todd's face, and now that he was closer, he saw the wounds in his temples. The scalpels that woman used left deep cuts where the knives had been plunged into the student's head.

Or maybe the scalpels weren't used at all. Art remembered Peter's head and the wounds he saw form without her needing to use the surgical blades.

"Todd? What's going on?" Art didn't think he'd really get an answer, but doing something, anything, helped to draw his focus away from the excruciating pain thrumming though his body.

Todd shook Art and turned him around. Art's surprise jumped between the number of other men and women – probably other students – underneath the Blackstone, all bleeding from the sides of their heads, and the fact that he was now standing in an open space that looked like something out of an old black-and-white movie, like one of those detective movies his Uncle Lorenzo used to watch when he would babysit Arturo when he was little.

Dusty wooden desks had been pushed against the walls, showing the large room to be about the size of what Art knew to be the main floor of the Blackstone. An old telephone sat on one of the desks, covered in cobwebs and mold. Rickety folding chairs lined one of the walls. A five-bladed ceiling fan missing two of its blades limply hung from the middle of the ceiling.

Art looked to Todd again. "What is this?"

"He can't hear you, Arturo." Stillborn pushed her way through a cluster of standing students. "I expected you to run away." Her eyes looked him up and down, and then she smiled. "Well, hobble away, anyway."

Now visible through the throng of stuck students, Art could see an open office door with a broken glass window. In that office was another man, this one clearly not a student or, at least, not someone who'd had their temples destroyed by whatever Stillborn was doing, sitting behind a desk that was slightly larger than those in this main room. Clearly looking for something, he was opening and closing the desk's drawers.

"Hey. Arturo." Stillborn made a point of blocking his site. "Look at me." She brought up both hands. She held a scalpel in each of them. "Should we finish what we started?"

Todd shook Art when he didn't answer.

"Luann!" The man at the office desk stood. "I can't find a key!"

Stillborn/Luann rolled her eyes. "Hold on a moment, Arturo." She turned and stomped back to the office.

Art tried to listen but the off-melody throbbing in his ears muffled whatever argument the two were starting to have.

Todd would not let Art relax. He held him stiff and straight, and even when Art tried to shift his weight, Todd shook him to keep him standing still. Art's back was sore, and he could feel his shoulders starting to ache. His right hip and leg felt like they were burning, but Todd wouldn't let him even just stand on one foot to alleviate the pain.

Luann walked back to Art, this time with the man from the office. The man did not look pleased.

"What are you doing with him, Luann?"

"I was turning him into one of my Born Again until you interrupted me by calling me down here. You said you found it."

He shrugged. "But I didn't say I could open it."

Luann's fists tightened around her scalpels. "Fine. Call Father."

The man lifted his open hands as if to make a point. "With what?"

Luann looked back to Art. "Do you have a phone?"

Art could barely shake his head.

"Fine." She stepped away from him and toward the center of the room. The students all turned their bodies to face her. Even Todd finally shifted his position to face Luann as she began to address them all.

"Empty your pockets, children."

Art felt Todd's hands loosen and release him. He immediately tried to shift his weight to his good leg, but he'd been standing too still for too long, and he fell to the floor.

The man Luann had been speaking with looked down at Art and sighed. "You're useless."

The students all began turning out their pants pockets, their jacket pockets, any pockets they might have had. Luann watched as coins, watches, brushes and combs, lighters, balls of paper, and old receipts all clattered on the aged tiled floor.

None of that drew Luann's attention, though. Instead, her eyes landed on one of the iPhones now on the floor.

Luann looked back to her partner. "There. Now call him."

Art watched the man reach for the phone. It was several feet away, too far for him to reach, and he made no effort to actually move closer to it. Instead, a pale orange light enveloped his hand.

And incredibly, the iPhone moved.

Sitting on the floor, Art watched as the iPhone grew liquid-like legs, stood upright, and begin walking toward him. It grew animation-like arms and marched. Art almost forgot about how much it hurt to try to stand while he walked this phone approach.

"No. Hold on." The man put a hand on Art's shoulder to hold him down. "Wait."

Art stopped struggling to stand. He had no choice. He waited.

When the iPhone was within arm's length, the man's hand closed around Art's shoulder.

"Pick it up and give it to me."

Art tried to move away, but this man's grasp prevented that.

"Do it."

The iPhone took a few final steps closer to Art before laying flat on its back. Its little legs and arms flowed back into its rectangular shape.

Art reached out to the phone and gingerly picked it off the ground.

It felt like a normal iPhone, and definitely not like something that had somehow sprung to life and sauntered over to him.

Art raised the phone. The man took it in both hands, releasing Art. Art pushed himself to get away, but Luann pointed a scalpel at him.

As she approached, she passed the scalpel to her other hand. She reached for Art to help him stand.

"What is happening?" Art looked from Luann to the man with the phone and back again. And then back to the man with the phone when he realized that the man's hands were both now glowing that sickly orange as he concentrated.

Luann tapped a foot. "Well? Are you calling him, Jon?"

Jon's attention snapped to Luann. "I'm trying to unlock the phone."

"Just hurry. I want to tell Father about Arturo."

"Who?"

"Arturo. This young man here."

"Why don't you finish turning him into one of your playthings."

"I got an idea while he was writhing around on the floor."

The man with the phone – Jon – let his hands stop glowing. He scowled at Luann. "What?"

A coarse smile flashed across Luann's face. "I think he'd make a good Hound." She looked down at Art. "Are you going to let me help you up?"

Art didn't want her help. He didn't want anything to do with her, or Jon, or this hidden basement in the Blackstone. He didn't want to be with these other students, he didn't want to be on the floor, he didn't want to be bleeding from his temples.

And he just didn't want to hurt anymore.

He reluctantly took Luann's hand and let her pull him upright.

Jon went back to working with the iPhone. "There. Finally." He punched a number into the phone, and brought it to his face.

Luann led Art toward the wall with the wooden chairs. "Here." She picked one from the wall, examined it, tossed it aside, and grabbed another. "This one seems solid enough." She opened it and set it behind Art.

He cautiously sat. The wood creaked and he could feel the chair legs spread slightly, but it remained solid, and Art let himself deeply exhale.

Art tried to watch Jon on the phone, but was unnerved as the other students all turned to face him. No, it wasn't him. It was her.

Luann stepped in front of him, completely blocking his view. "You'll like Father Override. He'll fix those." She reached out with her free hand and tapped the side of his head where she had attacked him earlier. "And he'll fix this." She patted his right knee. He braced himself as each tap on his bad leg sent waves of electric heat to his hip.

Jon dropped the phone. "Father Override will be here soon." Art leaned to the side and watched the phone, half expectingly it to grow legs and start walking again. "But you need to prepare a portal."

Luann looked at Art and shrugged before looking back at the

students. They all watched her, waiting on her words. She stepped among them, and finally turned to face Todd. "You. To the wall."

Todd launched into a sprint, and did not slow down before ramming his body, headfirst, into the concrete wall directly opposite Art.

Todd's head hit the solid wall first with a thud. Then a crunch. Then a sickening splat as the student took a step back and slammed his body again and again into the crumbling wallpapered walls.

Art looked back at Luann and Jon. In that moment, maybe in an attempt to distract himself from the sound of Todd destroying his body against a wall, Art realized the two of them shared some facial features. They had the same dark brown hair, the same cheek bones, the same green colored eyes. The same dark circles beneath those eyes. Jon even wore a similar windbreaker.

The sound of Todd's body smacking against the wall moistened with every thud. When Art finally looked back, he was immediately grateful Todd faced away from him. Even though he couldn't see his face, he could see hair and blood and other viscous chunks splatting around where Todd's softening face and body kept colliding against the solid wall.

Art wanted to stand, but his legs refused to work. Clamps of agony kept him in his chair.

Todd took several steps back, and flung himself against the wall again. Art flinched every time Todd smashed into it. He tried to look away, but only long enough to see Luann and Jon just standing there, watching this student destroy himself.

There was another thick crunch when Todd hefted his bulk one final time. He slid, face against the wall, leaving a red smear of blood, teeth, hair, and bone trailing to the floor. When Todd finally came to rest, the crimson mark on the wall began glowing.

At first, it was red, like all that blood, but as it brightened, it burned orange, then yellow, then back to red.

But it wasn't a blood red like before. Instead, it was a red the color of fire.

Even from where he sat, Art could feel the heat emanating from that streak on the wall.

He thought he heard someone chuckle – it might have been Jon – when fire burst from the marked wall. The flames extended a few feet, forcing the students nearby to take a few steps away from it, all while facing Luann.

The fire curled outward and around as if they were flaming fingers, and somehow found purchase on either side of the glowing red streak. And then they were more than fingers. Art watched as they each became large fully formed hands that begin pressing against the edges of the dripping sizzling remains of Todd.

Art saw those hands were coming from somewhere, somewhere beyond the walls of this abandoned basement, somewhere beyond the foundation and the structure of the building itself. As the burning hands moved apart, the wall easily split further open with them exposing old building material, wires, and pipes. Todd's body fell halfway into this newly formed portal and caught fire.

It was definitely Jon laughing at this point.

When the opening was wide enough for a man to pass through it, that was exactly what happened.

He was easily six feet tall, but walked with a confidence that seemed to add at least another foot to that. His sharp black suit absorbed some of the light of the room. His eyes were lit with fire, and his thick goatee seemed to smoke but not burn.

The hands of fire slid back into the wall. The man stepped over Todd's body and approached Jon.

Jon raised his hands defensively before the man could say anything. "Hey, she wanted me to call you."

Luann closed the distance between herself and this new arrival. The students continued to turn and face her. She shot a disapproving look at Jon before addressing the man.

"I think I have a new recruit."

"You think?" Father Override looked past Luann and at Art.

Despite the burning body on the other side of the room, despite the fire coming from wherever this Father Override came from, Art's body went cold when their eyes met.

Father Override moved toward Art. His steps were smooth, his footfalls made no sound. When he reached Art, he looked down at him. Art expected a look of pity, but instead, Father Override gave him a reassuring smile.

"You might be useful." He spun and turned back to Luann. "Stillborn, move your Born Again in front of the portal. We'll use them to house some of the demons bound to my service."

Art blinked and shook his head. "Demons?"

Luann nodded back at him. "And you'll get one, too. You'll be even stronger, you won't hurt anymore, you won't even need to think for yourself anymore, Arturo."

Art forced himself to stand, and he succeeded for just a moment. Then his knees just refused to work and he fell to the floor again.

Father Override sighed and continued to address Luann. "Pick him up and bring him to the portal. I'll be with your brother." Father Override gave Jon a commanding look. "You said you found it, Still Life?"

Jon/Still Life nodded. "In the office. There's a locked safe, and I'm sure it's in there."

"And you tried to move the safe?"

"It's built into the wall."

Father Override grabbed one of Stillborn's students. "Release this one to me. I need him to open the safe."

Stillborn slashed at the air with one of her scalpels.

The student Father Override had taken by the shoulder slumped, but remained standing. He blinked his eyes, reached up to feel the bloody sides of his head, and opened his mouth to scream.

But Father Override stopped him. "No." Father Override took the student by both shoulders and stared into his eyes. "No sounds. No cries. Just obedience."

The terrified student stood motionless as Father Override released him. He did as he was told and did not make any noise.

Which made it much easier for Art to hear the sizzling sound of scorching flesh when Father Override reached up and placed a forefinger in the middle of his forehead.

Stillborn helped Art to his feet, but he couldn't look at her. He could only watch Father Override. He thought he heard him tell the student to go with Still Life and use his hands to tear into the safe, but that didn't make any sense.

Nothing was making sense. Art let himself lean into Stillborn and she brought him closer to where Todd was slowly turning into ash. Where did her scalpels go? Why wasn't he hurting right now? There were more students here than normally lived in Blackstone. Who were all these people if they didn't live here? Could he reach the pickaxe? Was that another phone on the floor? A lighter? Who dropped all those pennies?

Stillborn surprised him when she gently let him sit down against the wall near Todd's remains. "You wait here." She turned and faced the students. "Line up. And prepare to receive greatness."

Those she had mesmerized did as they were told.

Stillborn stepped directly in front of the fiery portal, kicking Todd's remains into it to make room. She stared into the abyss for a moment before calling over her shoulder. "How many?"

Art tried to follow her gaze back to the office. Where he sat and the office door were not at an angle that let him see in, but Still Life poked his head out. "Father Override said you'd know when he had enough."

She gestured at the students lining up before her. "And if we have any of them left over?"

"Just toss them in. Oh, and make sure that guy you want as a Hound gets a good one."

She looked down at Art. "You see? Father Override agreed with me."

"I don't want . . . "

She frowned at him. "You don't want to hurt anymore. You don't want to keep letting anyone down. You don't want to struggle. And you won't. Not after you join us."

Stillborn looked back into the portal. "Well, you might not be you anymore. Not technically. Or you might be. I don't know. When my brother and I became Hounds for Father Override, he didn't use demons on us, so you'll have to let me know." She stepped to the side.

Art tried to lean over to look into the portal, but all he saw was fire and flame. The edges of the walls were smoking from the heat, the wallpaper peeled away in scorched curls, any exposed wiring seemed about to melt away and one exposed pipe was glowing a dull red.

Stillborn motioned for one of her Born Again students – a young woman wearing a pink polo with black slacks and still carrying a purse over her shoulder – to step in front of the portal. Stillborn whispered something in her ear, and for a moment, Art thought he saw real fear spread across the woman's face. Her eyes went wide, and she opened her mouth. Art assumed she meant to scream, but instead, a column of red flame and smoke shot out of the portal and into her face. It curled around her head several times before finally disappearing into her mouth.

The student jerked, and she finally dropped her purse.

Even from where he was sitting, Art felt the new heat radiating from her. And he could also hear the noises. Moans, shrieks, laughs, cries, and even part of a weird hymn somehow jumbled out of her body. He couldn't tell exactly where it was coming from because she was no longer still. She jerked back, and then Art heard another sound like something ripping.

And then he could see where this sound was coming from. The student's shoulders and neck thickened and grew. Her legs strained against her slacks as they also grew larger. Muscles seemed to inflate within her body, and her clothing would just not contain her anymore. Her hair fell away in smoldering clumps as her brow and head increased in size as well. Her skin blistered and turned a deep red color. The student finally just stood there, accepting her fate, even when what remaining clothing she had on caught fire.

Art pushed himself back from the wall and tried to crawl away.

CHAPTER 3

Four minutes before the explosion . . .

The transformed student stepped back and stomped toward the office. As soon as she was clear of the portal, the next student took her place. And the same thing happened. A third student. A fourth. The stench of burnt hair and hot metal filled the air.

Art's crawl came to a crunching end when a stern foot stomped down on his left hand. He winced and looked up to see Still Life peeking over a heavy wooden chest down at him. "Father says your turn is soon." He ground his heel into Art's fingers.

"Let him up." Father Override emerged from the office. On the floor, Art could see the still body of the student called into the office earlier. The dead student had a bloody stump where one of his hands should be.

Still Life stepped away and made room for Stillborn to pull Art up. Despite all this time she'd been pushing him and pulling him around the room, it just now occurred to him she didn't seem to struggle. He was a large guy, a former football player, and she looked like a 30-something-year-old woman no stronger than his Aunt Zoe. But here she was, ragdolling him and pushing him to . . . was he really her father? Was it a nickname or some sort of super-whatever codename? He certainly wasn't be a priest, a real priest?

Father Override reached him and took the hand Still Life had crushed. He massaged it, and the pain in his cracked fingers melted away. Art took his hand back. He made a fist, briefly considered swinging it at someone, anyone, but Father Override surprised him when he reached out to touch his temples.

The wounds in the sides of his head had stopped actively hurting at some point, but they still pulsed to his hammering heartbeat. But Father Override's fingers found the cut skin and pressed slightly. "I want you whole when you become a vessel."

The heat, the pressure, the residual pain all left his head. Father Override withdrew his hands. "There."

Stillborn motioned at Art's right leg. "His knee is wrecked."

Father Override gave her a questioning look.

She shook her head. "I didn't do it. It was like that before." She looked at Art. "Wasn't it, Arturo? Tell him."

Art weakly nodded.

Father Override turned that questioning look on Art. "How?"

Art's dry throat threatened to close. The air was getting thicker, hotter, and it was harder to breathe. "Football." His voice cracked in the heat.

The man in the black three-piece suit nodded. "Then we'll correct that, too."

The fifth and sixth transformed students to receive whatever the portal was offering had moved back toward the office. Father Override nudged Art along. "And you won't hurt anymore, Arturo."

He didn't want to move. He didn't want whatever Father Override was offering, but his feet slid forward anyway. Art reached at another student to steady himself, but his hands slipped. He felt his waist turn to lead the rest of his body to face the portal.

Through squinted eyes, Art saw into the flames beyond the opening. Angry yellow and orange fire screamed painful light along the edges, and just beyond the flames he saw throbbing sponge-like rocks creating a sort of tunnel. At the end of that tunnel, Art saw smoke.

And it was forming into a snake-like tube as it moved toward him.

Art was at the portal's edge now. He tried to look away, but he couldn't. His feet, his legs, his hips refused to move. With a grunt, he forced his arms up to press against the rim of the hole in the wall. The wall's concrete and stone crumbled in his hands. A burning wire cut into his left palm. He felt acrid smoke force itself in his mouth that he couldn't close. His vision doubled and then blurred.

Over his own screaming, he could still hear Father Override. "You won't be like the others. You'll be special, Arturo. Host to an incredibly strong demon. Not just a mindless drone like the others. I'm choosing you to be one of my hounds with Luann and Jon."

In contrast to the foul heat bombarding him from the portal, Father Override's breath was cool on his ear. "And you will be whole. More whole than you've ever been."

Art's gums dried and his teeth actively ached. He felt hot metal melt from a filling and sizzle on his papery tongue.

The smoke, the energy encircling his head and flooding his mouth filled his body with feverish heat. He felt his lungs expanding as his chest grew. His shirt stretched at the shoulders and around his arms as they swelled. His shoes felt like clamps on his toes and feet.

His ears rang, and he thought Father Override was pulling on them. Something in his skull made a cracking sound. A violent rush of agony ran down his spine. He tried to push away, he tried to shake his head free, but where would he go? He couldn't see anymore.

He tried to move his arms or his hands, but only his fingers would move. Art wiggled them and thought his fingernails would shake free. But he kept them moving, trying to find something to hold on to, some purchase to resist whatever was happening to him. His belt snapped free as his torso continued to expand. His right hand skidded along the edge of the portal and landed on something cylindrical and very hot.

And then, something exploded.

CHAPTER 4

Pentacle lay on her back, her coat torn open, her dark green costume smoldering, and her left elbow feeling like it was on fire. She blinked her eyes, tried to ignore the ringing in her ears, and sat up. Her coat was ruined, but the reinforced neoprene fabric that made up the majority of her field uniform seemed to be intact. She'd certainly hear about it later from Grandfather when they got back home and he saw the burns, but they were minor.

And she could still do her job.

She heard Voodoo Cowboy stirring to her right. He'd somehow managed to twist away from the concussive blast and was face down on the ground. His jacket protected most of his body as well, but like her, his arms were exposed and smoldering.

She patted her upper arms and wrist to make sure nothing was actively burning before getting to her feet. Pentacle noted Revenant was still sanding. He must have let himself lose his form as the force wave hit, keeping him from being knocked off his feet.

Voodoo Cowboy was coughing to clear his lungs when Pentacle reached him. She checked to make sure nothing of his was burning, and when satisfied, she helped him to his feet. Even before he was standing, he was flexing his hands again to re-manifest his revolvers.

Pentacle looked back to Revenant. "We're good. Go."

Revenant said nothing, shifted his khopesh from one hand to the other, and ran toward Blackstone Hall.

Voodoo Cowboy started to follow, but Pentacle grabbed his arm. "I need you out here. Look around."

Patches of grass were burning, but that's not what she was referring to. Students, teachers, and passersby needed their help. Some were laying on the ground, or sitting, or trying to get to their feet. Others were running away, and as if downtown Portland not having been designed for traffic wasn't bad enough, now cars and other vehicles were scrambling to get away from the burning building.

Voodoo Cowboy gave her a quick salute after he let one of his guns disappear, and went to the closest person – an older woman limply holding an empty dog leash – to help her.

Abigail sighed and took a moment to steady herself. Her ears still whined, especially whenever she turned her head to the left. The nearest person who looked like they needed help sat on the grass several feet away. A two-foot-long skid in the ground told Abigail the young man must have been pushed back by the blast. She ran to him, letting what remained of her jacket fall off her body.

The young man – maybe a high school student – sat still, staring in the direction of the Blackstone. He didn't react when Pentacle reached him. She was grateful for that. Sometimes the people she was trying to help reacted poorly when she started using magic directly in front of them.

She stepped before the high school student, blocking his view of the burning building. He didn't react. With practiced grace, she let her hands swim through the air. Her fingertips tingled and she smiled. She felt the slightest pressure in her eyes, knowing they were glowing a soft green light as she pulled at the magic within her. The gem embedded in the center of the chest of her costume also glowed. Whenever she wasn't actually using her magic, she liked to imagine that her long red hair flailed around her head as if she was standing in front of a fan for the most dramatic effect. But in the field, when sometimes even seconds counted, she didn't have time to think about her hair.

She only thought about the magic and how she could use it to help people.

Pentacle brought the bottom edge of her palms together with her fingers splayed out and upward. She then brought her wrists down but kept her hands together. A whispering bolt of heavy green jumped from within her, out from her chest, through her arms and into her palms, and finally leaving her and hitting the stunned student.

The energy encompassed him.

And Pentacle felt him go to sleep.

Satisfied that she'd successfully put the student into magical stasis, she left him to look for more people to help.

She didn't expect to see Voodoo Cowboy firing into the crowd of bystanders.

"What are you doing?"

For a moment, she wasn't sure if she could hear him, but after firing three more shots at people, he looked back at her. "Sleep dust. Special recipe."

He then took aim at another person – a teacher in a torn sports coat and grass-stained khakis – and fired. A burst of glittering dust filled the air around the teacher's head. The teacher gently lowered himself to the ground and closed his eyes.

Pentacle knew Grandfather wouldn't like that, but it got the job done. And if Voodoo Cowboy kept at it, he could take over the job of helping the witnesses and victims long enough for her to contact her grandfather and fill him in.

She let her left hand float to the side of her head and with her first two fingers, strummed the helix of her ear. Her vision blurred for a moment, and then she was mentally linked to her grandfather.

"Abigail? Are you okay?"

She heard his words. They sounded distant with a slight echo, but she heard them. She thought her response back to him.

I'm fine. Do you know what happened? What's happening now?

"I can see it."

She didn't expect that. *How?*

"It's already on social media."

Pentacle didn't break the magical telepathic connection, but did scan the scene around her. Voodoo Cowboy was still using his revolvers to gently put victims and bystanders to sleep. Men, women, the occasional child, and even a Scottish terrier slept, dotting the smoldering field of burnt grass and chunked asphalt around Blackstone Hall. It took another moment, but she spotted a woman with short blonde hair and a black-and-white checkered coat holding up her phone.

Abigail waved at the woman with the phone. The woman awkwardly waved back.

"I can see you now."

We're helping with the civilians. I don't think there were any casualties outside, but we'll know for sure later. Revenant went inside what's left of the Blackstone.

"Revenant isn't with you? Who is this 'we'?"

He didn't give her a chance to think an answer back to him.

"Oh. Wait. Nevermind. I can see him in the Facebook video."

Voodoo Cowboy happened to be in the area. You two really should talk.

Her grandfather moved on. "If he's helping outside, you should assist Revenant. The explosion wasn't the end of it."

Can you still not tell what kind of magic we're dealing with?

"Sadly, no. It feels . . . ancient and dark. Be careful."

I always am, Grandfather.
Her grandfather broke the telepathic connection.

CHAPTER 5

Even though it had been over a century since he'd been turned into . . . whatever it was he was now, Hence Williams still sometimes struggled to maintain his solid form. The breathing and meditation techniques Deacon Andrews had taught him over the years certainly helped, but when in the field, it was still a challenge, especially when he had his khopesh in hand.

The Egyptian sword was the first artifact he found in that ancient Egyptian tomb, and it was the only one he would be able to take out with him. When he broke the seal barring the tomb of Necherôphes, when that cacophonous blast of raw energy and ages-old dust and ash tore into him and ripped part of his humanity away, it was all he could hold onto.

The century-old memories gnawed at him. He doubted himself, his actions, all the choices he made in his life before running way to Egypt. No matter how hard he tried, even if they did help with maintaining his solid form, the meditations always brought all those memories and regrets to the forefront of his mind.

It didn't help that the doorway leading into Blackstone Hall was flanked by a pair of generic Egyptian-style relief sculptures. He didn't know him to joke, but when Deacon told him and Abigail where they needed to be, Hence thought the leader of Solemn Judgment was teasing him.

Deacon assured him he was not.

The busts were significantly damaged in the blast. One spread across the ground in stone chunks. The other, mostly intact, stared up at him as he stepped past it and over a chunk of burning door.

When the fire first bellowed out of the building, Hence somehow managed to keep his form unsubstantial enough for the force to pass through him. But now that he'd had time to think about what he was doing, he needed to reserve part of his mind to remain focused on staying intangible.

But just in case, he still made sure to step over and around any flaming debris.

Surprisingly, the floors above the first hadn't come tumbling

28

down. The blast seemed to direct itself down and out the front doorway of the hallway Hence now found himself in. He continued further down the hall, stepping over broken glass, large pieces of concrete, and the remains of a foul-smelling burning cork board.

Apart from an obviously dead young man in what was left of the lobby, Hence didn't see any other victims. Or remains. Had they all been lucky that there weren't any other students or staff in the blast area?

No, they weren't lucky. Just by thinking that, Hence realized he may have just jinxed the team when he spotted movement at the end of what would have been the central hallway. Hence quickened his pace, let his khopesh dissolve into nothingness so he had his hands free, and tried to think of anything other than Egypt so he could be solid enough to help whoever had survived the explosion.

A twisted bit of torn tile caught the edge of his jacket. It tugged him as he moved further into the Blackstone. He was solid enough.

He shook himself free, and went toward whoever survived. As he got closer, he could make out a hole in the floor at the end of what used to be the hallway. Smoke chugged out of that opening. The hole might have been the result of the explosion, but that didn't matter right now. What mattered was the pair of hands trying hold on to its edge.

"I'm right here." He reached down. "Grab my hand."

One of those hands reached up and took his. And it felt wrong.

And now that Hence was closer, he could tell it looked wrong, too. Maybe it was the result of a burn, but the flesh was rough and the wrong color. Its skin was blood red, and instead of trying to pull up and out of the hole, it tried to pull Hence down into it.

Hence took a quick breath and let his body lose its solidity. Sometimes it was easy to make that transition, and he was thankful for it now as those thick crimson hands slipped through his own.

They grabbed for the edge of that hole. Once they found it, the owner of those hands yanked himself up.

Hence stepped back, passing through flaming debris and books. The red-handed being that emerged didn't look like a student. He didn't even look human.

He was hairless and Hence could tell he was a he because he was also naked. The man looked more like a swollen bodybuilder than anything else save for the flicking tale trailing behind him.

The flicking devil's tail? Hence blinked. It looked like something out a cartoon.

This hairless-man-devil thing locked eyes with Hence. Hence saw no pupils, no other color than blinding yellow in its eye sockets, but yet he still knew this creature was looking at him. It then worked its mouth open and an acidic growl spilled out of it.

Even though he wasn't solid, Hence still shuddered before he focused to bring his khopesh sword back. He started cursing himself for sending his weapon away in the first place, but he was interrupted when the creature launched a hefty fist at his face.

It passed straight through Hence's head, but it was still very much there. It felt like scalding leather pushing through his nose and into his brain. He shouldn't have felt anything, and he'd talk with Deacon about it later, but for now he quickstepped back to keep that thing from hitting him again.

Hence shook his head and brought up his sword. He never learned how to use the sword properly, mostly because it wasn't a proper sword, not anymore. It could have been an actual weapon at some point, or maybe something used strictly for ceremony or decoration before Hence got his hands on it. Now, it was what he would use to defend himself against this hairless, eyeless, clothesless slab rushing him.

He ducked and swung as the creature closed on him. When the sword made contact with the thing's legs, it slowed down, but still passed through them. Hence started to question why there was any resistance at all. It should have just stunned the creature. That's what his khopesh was supposed to do.

The creature was not stunned. It snorted at him in defiance.

Hence ran backwards to get away from it.

Another creature, equally muscular, hairless, and naked, pulled itself out of the hole.

His khopesh in one hand, Hence reached down with his other to grab a chunk of smoldering cinderblock leaning against a piece of wall. He willed his hand to pass through it and then into it, changing its mass to match his own weightlessness. Hence flung it as hard as he could. When it left Hence's hand, its weight returned, and it smashed into the closest creature's chest.

It crumbled against the thing's hardened body.

Hence turned to run, but not before he thought he saw a third creature, just as red and devil-tailed as the others, yank itself up from underneath Blackstone Hall.

Hence could hear gunshots outside the wreckage of the building. He assumed it was just Voodoo Cowboy using those guns of his for some reason. Whatever the reason was, it meant he would be too busy to help Hence deal with these things stomping after him.

He couldn't see Pentacle, and then realized it would probably be best to keep these things contained inside the actual wreckage anyway. Leading them outside would make them harder to corral and deal with. He took a deep breath and turned to face them.

Again, he took a heavy leather fist to the face.

And this time, it pushed him back several feet.

Hence struggled to keep his balance and slashed with the sword. It just passed weakly through the creature's torso, but that was it. It left no mark and dealt no damage. He looked into the creature's fiery non-eyes and braced himself for another punch.

"Revenant! Get down!"

Hence did not turn to see who was yelling his name, but he recognized her voice.

And he did exactly what Pentacle told him to do.

He had barely made it into a crouching position before a vivid green beam fired over his head with a loud shracking sound.

The blast hit the creature in the chest, pushing it back into the one behind it. They both slid back several feet before their mouths opened in unison.

The sound of their combined screams tore through the air like a rusted cannon. It burned Hence's nose and rang his ears as he stood there, facing them.

Pentacle moved to his side. Hence lifted his khopesh defensively and barely tilted his head toward his teammate. "How are things out there?"

"Voodoo Cowboy has it under control, and emergency services are on the way." Pentacle brought her hands in front of her chest and made two tight fists. "What about these two?"

Hence wondered why the creatures hadn't started back toward them. He gestured with his sword past them. "There's an opening down that way. They came out of there, and I think there's a third one."

"Any idea what they are?"

The red monstrous creatures still hadn't advanced.

Hence shook his head.

Another heaving growl sounded from behind the two creatures. Pentacle and Revenant leaned to either side to see past them and saw two more just as broad and muscular and devilish as the others approaching their comrades.

"That's more than a third." Pentacle took a step forward. "We can't keep fighting in here. The building's not stable." She extended her arms to her sides, completely blocking Revenant behind her. "I'll draw them out, but you should check for any other survivors."

"Are you sure? You want them out there with the bystanders."

"I told you Voodoo Cowboy has that handled." Her fists disappeared in a mass of light and magic. "Survivors, Revenant."

He nodded even though Pentacle had her back to him. Closing his eyes, he focused on his breathing. He tried to feel his surroundings, and let the air in his lungs slowly leave his body. How his insubstantial form was able to keep air in his lungs he didn't understand, but that didn't matter now. Being present in the moment, in the world, and letting it all pass through him was all that needed to matter.

As did any other survivors in the building.

He let his eyes slide open to see Pentacle approaching the creatures before her. Her uniform, her entire body, was glowing green which Revenant knew meant she was drawing on a great deal of her magic. She was an extremely powerful caster and would be all right on her own.

Probably.

She better be. He didn't want to answer to her grandfather if something happened to Abigail in the field.

He put those distracting thoughts aside and took one more deep breath. His khopesh sword faded, and his body followed suit.

Gravity slowly forgot about Hence. He floated from the floor, and instead of colliding with the ceiling, he easily passed through it. Through the darkness of solid steel, concrete, and tile he continued to rise until his head crested the second story. He let himself continue to float higher until his boot bottoms were parallel with the floor.

He snapped himself solid and felt the floor beneath him. There was no power, but plenty of open windows and damaged walls let enough light in from outside. Hence immediately began searching what was left of the rooms. That there wasn't more damage to the building even just here on the second floor was a pleasant surprise, and it made his search easier. He didn't need to navigate too much rubble and debris, just several doors knocked out of their frame and an uneven layer of broken glass and chunks of paint.

Shrack! Even one floor up, Hence heard Pentacle blasting away at those creatures. She was strong. There were four of them against one of her, but he'd seen her face a pack of frenzied, frothing werewolves just last year and she walked away with barely a scratch.

But what if there were more than four?

He'd just have to work faster so he could rejoin her at the bottom level.

But what about what was underneath the bottom level? Deacon didn't say Blackstone Hall had a basement. Where were those creatures coming from?

After clearing the second floor and finding no one, he began his steady breathing routine again. He stretched for another moment of calm, ignoring the sounds of fighting below, allowing himself to float to the third floor.

The further up Hence went in Blackstone Hall, the less the building seemed to have suffered any damage at all from the explosion. A framed bulletin board had been knocked loose, its glass spread like pebbles across the floor, but otherwise, there was very little evidence of the building suffering any trauma.

The student residences' doors were all open, as they were on the floor below. Hence quickly moved from room to room, checking for survivors or victims. It was easier for him to pass through the rooms' shared walls instead of going in one door, turning around, going out, taking a few steps and doing it all over again. He made it down one side of the building before turning back to check the other side.

And he finally found someone.

A young woman lay in a crumpled heap near the foot of her bed. Clothes, books, and a couple of pillows lay strewn around the room. One of those pillows had been torn open, its stuffing stretched from a bedpost to the woman's still clutched hand.

Hence solidified his form and knelt beside her. He gently brushed her dark blonde hair away from her face to reveal her open eyes trapped in a face full of frozen fear and confusion. Two drying tracks of blood trailed down either side of her face. He cradled her head in his arms, and noted the wounds near her ears. They were deep, and made cleanly with something quite sharp.

He lightly brushed his fingers across her eyes, closing her eyelids, before lifting her and placing her on the bed, making sure to free the remains of the pillow from her hand. Whatever cut into her head, into her scalp, had to have been strong enough to puncture her skull. That's the only way wounds like this would have killed her, right?

Hence would try to answer that question later. For now, he had more work to do.

Blackstone Hall was a five-story building, and even cheating by passing through walls and floors, Hence still felt it took too long to check the other rooms for any other survivors.

Unfortunately, he found none. Instead, he found six more victims, all with similar wounds at their temples, all cold and dead. Hence did what he could for them out of respect, placing their bodies on nearby beds, and closing their eyes.

What killed them, how that answer might be related to whatever those things were crawling out of the basement, and why there weren't any more students or staff in the building were questions he'd have to come back to to answer.

He let his mind drift, and his body lost its form again. Dropping through the floors and ceilings and floors again, he willed himself to fall faster. He lost track of when he stopped hearing the sounds of fighting or Pentacle's aggressive magic earlier, but when it occurred to him, Hence pushed himself hard to the ground floor. He flexed his right hand, ready to manifest his sword as soon as he landed.

Floor through ceiling, dropping to the next floor, Hence finally put the first level directly beneath his feet. He was in a corner of the building whose outside wall still stood, but the interior was an open space of blasted rubble. How much of that rubble came from the initial explosion versus the collateral damage Pentacle and her opponents had caused Hence couldn't tell. He'd ask her, when she was done fighting the – he took a moment to count the bodies – fifth monster. It, too, looked like the others with its deep crimson skin, hairless body, and angry eyes.

Pentacle was on one knee, her back to him. Hence knew his teammate well enough to know she had to be exhausted. If she'd been fighting this entire time, using that much magic would have worn her down.

The creature bellowed a sound that grated against Hence's ears. It didn't seem to care that Pentacle might have had enough. It lifted its meaty fists, lowered its head, and started a weighty march toward Pentacle.

Hence saw Pentacle wasn't moving. He could tell she was breathing, but she wasn't standing. She wasn't taking a defensive position. She wasn't doing anything.

The creature was several feet away from her. Hence was further away than that, but that thing was slow moving.

Hence ran.

Pentacle still didn't move as he closed the distance, shortening the imaginary line connecting himself, Pentacle, and the creature. She still wasn't moving.

The creature grunted another belch as it continued its march.

"Pentacle!" She didn't look up when he shouted her name. "Abby!"

She still just knelt between him and the creature.

If he pushed himself just a bit more, he'd reach Pentacle before their opponent did. He briefly considered bearing the khopesh, but held off when Pentacle's head suddenly snapped up.

He was just feet away.

The creature was a bit further away than that.

Pentacle suddenly stood.

Hence forced his body to go intangible just as he reached Pentacle, but he didn't stop running. He passed through her from behind, didn't think about what that felt like or the green-goo-like light that suddenly clung to his body, and as soon as he was on the other side of his teammate, he went solid again, manifested his sword, and swung at the now-stunned creature.

He willed his sword solid as it dug deep into the creature's chest, splitting straining skin and hard muscle. Bright glowing liquid spilled from the slice, splattering the ground and bursting into tiny flames.

The creature grabbed at its chest and screamed at Hence.

Hence drew back his sword for another swing.

And another creature – one even larger than the one directly in front of him – appeared in the space behind him. It leapt into the air, almost scraping the ceiling. For an absurd moment, it seemed to float.

Hence quickly noted several differences between this new creature and the other ones they'd been fighting.

It was even bigger, if that was possible. It still had human-like eyes instead of fiery pits, and even had black hair. Most notable, however, were its elongated ears and burnt-white horns sprouting from its head.

And it held a pickaxe.

It came down pickaxe first just behind the hairless one, driving the tool into that one's skull. The pickaxe sunk deep into its head with a chunking sound. Thick blood and fire spurted from the wound.

The hairless creature flailed its arms around its head, but could not reach the pickaxe before it crumpled to the floor in front of the two members of Solemn Judgment.

Hence exchanged a look with Pentacle before the horned being in front of them also collapsed.

CHAPTER 6

Heavy breaths heaved out of this new creature as it lay in front of them. It also had that obvious devil tail the others hand, but Hence couldn't help but keep noting its differences. Hair. Horns. Those ears. And did it just help them?

"Do you think you can pick it up?" Pentacle was starting to move like herself again.

Hence bent down and pulled on its arm. Its skin was hot and rough, like boiled pigskin, and it was heavy.

He looked back at Pentacle. "Maybe."

"Make it happen." She seemed to suddenly remember to scowl at him. "Then we'll talk." She turned and made her way back outside.

Hence didn't have to think long to know she meant talking about his passing through her. That's not something they ever practiced, and if he was being honest with himself, he didn't know if it would even work.

That was not going to be fun conversation. Even though he was several decades older than her, even older than her grandfather, she still made him feel like the spoiled rich kid his parents scolded whenever he did or said anything they considered "not befitting a Williams." That was a long time ago, but Pentacle was somehow able to bring those feelings back when she looked like this. She clearly was upset, and he knew he'd hear about it.

That would happen later, though. Now, Hence continued to pull at the creature's arm. He slowly dragged him toward the front of what was left of Blackstone Hall, hoping there wouldn't be any more of these things – hairless or otherwise – coming after him.

Portland's emergency services were already on the scene. As Hence pulled his captive away from the building, he saw Voodoo Cowboy talking with a young woman who was recording him with her cell phone. That wasn't going to earn him any points with Deacon, he knew, but he didn't think Voodoo Cowboy really cared all that much.

Pentacle was talking with two EMTs. She might have been explaining how they managed to put so many of the bystanders outside to sleep, or maybe how to revive them.

Hence kept pulling, but stopped when Pentacle finally made a point of looking in his direction.

She gestured at the library next door, didn't wait for him to respond, and made her way to where they were when the explosion first happened.

Hence nodded and fought the temptation to curse Abby for not helping him.

Her face had barely softened when he finally joined her. The thing he almost disgracefully dragged behind him never woke. Hence even thought he heard it snoring.

Pentacle had a blanket she'd taken from the back of one of the ambulances, and draped it over the creature's naked body, offering it a modicum of dignity. Then she locked eyes with Hence.

Hence realized she was waiting for him to say something. "Abby, I don't know what's wrong."

"We're in the field."

"Fine. Pentacle. What's wrong?"

She glowered at him, and for a moment, he thought her eyes started glowing. Finally, she sighed. "When you . . . passed through me . . . I didn't realize that's what it felt like."

"What do you mean?" He moved closer to her. "Are you hurt?"

"No." She took a step back and gazed across downtown Portland's South Park Blocks. "It didn't exactly feel good, but I'm not hurt."

Hence nodded. "Good. Okay." He paused, and when she didn't continue, he pressed her. "What did it feel like?"

Pentacle looked back at him and began to answer, but cut herself short. This time, he was sure her eyes flashed with that green magical energy. Her attention went back to the Blackstone.

Hence followed her look. A man – this one with non-red skin and actually wearing some clothing – stood defiantly in what would have been the front entryway of the building. He set a large box on the ground before him and stared at the crowd.

Pentacle didn't look away, but tilted her head toward Hence. "Do you recognize him?"

Hence shook his head.

A police officer also took notice of the man standing in the rubble of Blackstone Hall's front door. "Sir? Are you okay?" The officer approached him with a helping hand.

The man grinned and knelt. A burst of orange light leapt from his hand into the ground. The police officer stepped back as the nearby debris and rocks also began to glow orange.

Pentacle was already moving back toward the Blackstone as larger pieces of the blasted building also began to glow. Then they began moving, jerking and rolling toward the man with the glowing orange hand.

The one remaining intact Egyptian pharaoh relief sculpture pulled itself from its resting place and slid across the ground toward him. And when all these pieces had reached him, the man stood and reached out to the rubble.

Hence began moving back toward the Blackstone himself as this form of rubble and debris slowly constructed itself between the man and the heroes. Chunks of plaster and concrete, glass, wood, even the remains of that dead student's backpack all coalesced into the shape of a large man. The Egyptian sculpture slid up its legs and chest, taking its place at the top as some sort of absurd head.

This new . . . thing moved awkwardly as it twitched forward. Pentacle was about to greet it head on. The man that had somehow weirdly built this impromptu golem turned and stepped back into what would have been the Blackstone's lobby. He bent and picked up the large wooden box. It looked familiar to Hence. What was it?

Shrack! A blast from Pentacle's outstretched hands slammed into the golem, pushing it back and knocking it over.

A quick glance showed Hence the police officers were drawing their weapons and aiming in Pentacle's direction. Voodoo Cowboy drew his magic revolvers as well, but instead of taking a defensive stance like the police, he charged.

Hence called forth his sword and did the same.

The golem put its feet beneath itself and leaned toward Pentacle. It loomed over her, and looked down at her with the eyes set in the pharaoh sculpture serving as its face. Hence saw where Pentacle's blast hit it in its chest.

It had barely made a dent.

Defeaning gunshots filled the air when Voodoo Cowboy fired as he approached. Chunks of stone and other burnt building material flaked off the golem's shoulders and neck wherever it was hit by whatever concoction Voodoo Cowboy was firing at it.

Hence joined the two other heroes in front of the golem, and lifted his khopesh. He swung for its head. The Egyptian face mocked him. The blade passed into it, and Hence quickly forced it to become solid. The ancient brass weapon took form inside the golem's structure. Hence continued his sword swipe, tearing half of the golem's head away from its somehow-animated body.

Voodoo Cowboy kept firing. Hence knew he wouldn't need to stop to reload.

Pentacle's left hand twitched, and a bubble of green light suddenly surrounded all three of them. The golem swung an uncoordinated hand at them, but it bounced off Pentacle's defensive shield. Voodoo Cowboy's charges were still able to pass through it, however, and continued to eat away at their opponent.

Hence brought his sword down in front of him, shoved it forward, and crotched the golem with the hooked end of the khopesh. He pulled up as hard as he could. The blade caught and pulled into its groin and torso. Hence grunted as he yanked the sword back.

Chunks of the golem tore free with the khopesh, but Pentacle's shield deflected them.

Voodoo Cowboy's guns stopped. Hence shot him a look and saw him muttering something over them, his eyelids fluttering. He couldn't make out what he was saying. Not over Pentacle's repeated blasts into the golem's chest.

Shrack! Shrack! SHRACK!

Hence swung again, returning his attack to the golem's head. He took the same approach as before, letting the sword pass into the golem, then solidifying it once inside, and pulling it free. This time, the entire Egyptian face came off and clattered in pieces against Pentacle's shield.

Voodoo Cowboy's eyes snapped open. He raised his guns, at least that's what Hence assumed he was doing. The ends of the man's arms were covered in obscuring darkness. Hence couldn't see the man's hands or weapons.

But he certainly heard the gunshots. They fired like thunderclaps, and this time, wherever the charges hit the golem, they exploded in bright flashes of light about the size of a baseball.

The three heroes continued to fight the monster as the police, and that student aiming her smart phone at them, stood back.

The golem frantically swung, and once even kicked, at them. Pentacle's shield kept them safe. Voodoo Cowboy's revolvers kept tearing away at it, sending golem bits and dust flying.

Hence kept slashing, letting the sword pass though upon entry but willing it solid halfway through the swing.

And then what was left of the diminishing golem simply came apart and crumbled in front of them.

Voodoo Cowboy stopped firing. Pentacle kept her shield in place.

Hence stepped forward and, with his foot, swept part of the golem's pieces away.

CHAPTER 7

Father Override stepped between the two giant hands of fire holding open the portal leading from the basement of Blackstone Hall and into the South Dome of Goldendale Observatory. Stillborn and Still Life followed, the former carrying her scalpels, the latter carrying the canopic chest they recovered from the building. Father Override ground his teeth, and glared at the siblings as he dismissed the portal with an abrupt snap of his fingers, leaving any surviving Born Again behind.

And Stillborn wasn't happy about it. "We left all of them behind."

Father Override resisted the urge to lash out at the young woman, to remind her of her place in their arrangement, to refresh her memory of who exactly gave her the ability to create so many Born Again zombies in the first place.

Instead, he chose to ignore her, and walked to the large 24-inch telescope. He rested his hand on cool metal of the step ladder leading up to its eyepiece. He'd accomplished the first step required to pay back his old friend when they recovered that chest.

He knew that waiting inside that chest were four canopic jars containing "the viscera of a god." Whatever that meant. It didn't matter, though. He didn't need to understand anything other than the promise he made so many years ago.

Thinking back to when he made that agreement, Father Override couldn't help but smile. It had been over a century, but the memory was as fresh as it would have been if that fateful meeting had happened only yesterday.

"The viscera of a god, the heart of a giant, and the skull of a child." That's what he made James promise in exchange for power, for this long life, for the ability to change people and convert them to his cause.

To become Father Override.

"Where do you want this?"

Father Override opened his eyes and looked back at the two siblings. "Put it in the utility room."

Still Life nodded and left the South Dome.

Stillborn lingered behind.

"If this is about your Born Again, you can make more. You will make more."

"It's not that."

"Then what?"

Stillborn looked in the direction her brother left and waited as if to make sure he couldn't hear. "I'm confused."

Father Override approached the young woman and placed his hands on her shoulders. "By what?"

"What happened?"

He let his hands fall away from her and back to his sides. Of the two, she questioned him more. Fortunately for her, she hadn't outwardly challenged him. Yet.

In response to her question, he'd give her a calculated answer. "One of you made a mistake."

"How?"

"That explosion was not supposed to happen."

"No."

"What was supposed to happen, then?"

Stillborn looked away. She lowered her voice. "We were supposed to get the chest and get out."

"And who changed the plan?"

"My brother and I are your only Hounds. I thought we could use another. That's why I wanted to call you."

He tightened his eyes and fixed his stare at her. "Do you think you're not capable of doing the job? Do you need help?"

She stiffened. "No."

"Then why?"

She didn't answer his question, but asked another of her own. "If you thought it was a bad idea, why did you even come when we called you?"

He shook his head. "When you changed the plan, I grew concerned, child." He emphasized that last word. That's what she was to him. They all were. The siblings, the guards and staff they overtook when they came to the observatory. All of them. Compared to himself, they were all young children in desperate need of controlling.

"You clearly needed guidance. And help. You should thank me again."

Still Born looked questioningly at him.

"How many times have you been spared death because of me,

Luann? I've lost count." He really hadn't. What happened at Blackstone Hall would mark this the seventh time he had to save the woman. Compared to her brother, she needed so much more instruction.

"It wasn't my fault."

He turned his back on her and reapproached the telescope. "You and your brother were to retrieve that box and that was it. I knew you would want to play, though, and I anticipated that."

He ascended the stepladder and rested his hand on the telescope's housing. The cool, uncaring metal helped to keep his rising anger at bay.

"I took what ability you had and increased it. I made it so you would not have to use those scalpels anymore. I expected you to get into the building with your brother, find that box, use whatever or whoever you had to get it for me, and leave."

"But I like my scalpels."

"They're messy. And they take time." He looked back at her. "Tell me about the one you thought I needed."

She looked confused.

"Tell me, Luann, about that young man you thought I needed as another Hound."

She slid her hands into her pockets. Father Override suspected she was grabbing those scalpels. How she didn't manage to cut herself he couldn't guess. Children were just lucky, he supposed.

"I just thought he could be helpful for whatever we're doing for you."

He nodded. "He was a good specimen, Luann. He would have made a good Hound. I sensed potential in him. There was so much pain and resentment in that young man."

Luann was nodding along now. "Yes! That's what I thought!"

Father Override frowned theatrically. "It is too bad the explosion killed him."

She stopped nodding. "And the rest of my Born Again."

"You still have some here, and you'll make more. I have a new task for you and your brother." He dismissed her. "Go. Be ready tomorrow morning for another trip to Portland."

When she hesitated, he glared at her, willing her to leave.

Finally, she did.

Alone in the South Dome, Father Override thought back to what had happened at Blackstone Hall. Yes, he did see some potential in the one she called Arturo. There was trauma there. He sensed it immediately, and Luann was right. He might have made a good addition as a Hound.

For now, though, he'd have to settle for the Heckler siblings. He barely saved them and himself from the explosion. Everyone else was killed when the basement of Blackstone Hall exploded.

CHAPTER 8

Arturo Banks was not killed when the basement of Blackstone Hall exploded.

Also, Deacon Andrews and the members of Solemn Judgment did not know the over eight-foot-tall crimson-skinned creature with the pointed ears, horn, and tail was Arturo Banks. When Pentacle and Revenant returned from Portland with this creature in tow, Deacon made sure he was covered with a blanket and placed comfortably in a quickly-prepared guest room.

Deacon was watching the events of the Blackstone Hall explosion through various streaming outlets, so he saw some of the fight that happened afterward. What happened inside the building, and how Abigail and Hence ended up with whatever or whoever was snoring down the hall from his office, he didn't know.

Yet.

He sat behind the large dark wood desk in the center of his office and research library. Deacon could watch streaming video or use the internet, but he liked the feeling of turning the pages of a book. And he had plenty of them. Books on magic, vampires, demons, sacrificial rites, a queer history of the history of cedar trees in America, two cookbooks, a collection of dead poetry, history, and so much more. His books were his sanctuary. His books were the basis of his real work leading Solemn Judgment.

And he had three of those on his desk right now. He'd been going through them, flipping through pages, quickly scanning for anything that might help them in identifying what they'd faced on the Portland State University campus. They didn't have a lot of information yet, but if he could get a jump on the research, it would save them time with the paperwork.

Deacon rubbed his forehead and pushed back in his chair. It wasn't Solemn Judgment's 6-week rotation, but video of their activity was online and the SRD would want to know what happened. He did not want to report anything about whoever or whatever they brought back with them from Portland yet, not until they knew what they were dealing with.

They hadn't yet done a proper debrief. In the short time since they'd returned courtesy of Pentacle's teleportation spell, they'd only been able to report back to him that the being they had in tow had helped them during part of the battle the cameras weren't able to see.

They also assured Deacon that Voodoo Cowboy was only helping.

It wasn't that Deacon disliked Troy Norris personally. He was registered according to the Nixon Protocols, and since he was based in Portland, Deacon found it incredibly easy to keep tabs on him from his home in Salem. Deacon knew Voodoo Cowboy did more good than harm. And he'd helped Solemn Judgment several times over the years, whether Deacon wanted him to or not.

He just did not like they way Norris manifested his magical abilities. Even at Blackstone Hall, he could be seen firing into the crowd with those guns of his. Despite assurances from his granddaughter, it just did not look safe. It did not look like something a hero would or should do.

Deacon chuckled to himself. Not that Solemn Judgment called themselves heroes. They were protectors.

And, more importantly, Deacon was his granddaughter's protector. He smiled at a framed photograph on one of the many bookshelves in the room. It was a black-and-white photo taken almost seventy years ago, and showed a much younger and uniformed Corporal Deacon Andrews holding his wife.

If being exposed so much to the Pentacle magic through his wife and her female descendants was going to extend his life the way that it had, he would use it to protect his family.

And that meant keeping an eye on people like Voodoo Cowboy or anyone else that acted recklessly around his granddaughter.

"Grandfather." Abigail entered the office and took one of the chairs opposite his from the desk. She'd changed out of her uniform and had her hair pulled back after taking a shower. "Hence is checking on our guest, but he'll be here soon."

"Very good." Deacon closed the open books on his desk and slid them to the side. "I'll be sending an after-action report in about an hour, and I'll need his statement."

Abigail nodded.

"But off the record, Abigail, how are you?"

"I'm not hurt."

Deacon felt his brows furrowing. "That's not what I meant. I couldn't make out what was said in the online videos, but it was clear to me you were upset."

She looked away from her grandfather. "I'm fine."

He shook his head. "I also felt something I've never felt before. Something happened in that building. Something with you and the Pentacle magic."

Abigail was trying to avoid his eyes, but failed. She looked up at her grandfather. "Hence did . . . something in the field he'd never done before."

"What did he do?" He tried to keep his voice calm and even, but if something happened to his granddaughter . . .

She stood and walked to one of the wall bookcases. She let a finger trail down the book spines and paused before lowering her voice. "He passed through me."

Before Deacon could respond, she quickly spun back to him. "He was helping me, maybe even saving me. But I'd never felt anything like that before."

"Can you describe it?"

Her eyes drifted. "There was a rush of heat, and everything went blurry. Not like there was something wrong with my eyes, but like there was something in front of them. Like something was obscuring my vision."

"And it only lasted for a moment?"

She nodded. "Just while Hence was . . . was moving through me."

"What else?"

Abigail winced. "It didn't hurt. Not really. And I'm fine now. I guess I've never thought about what happens to the people he does that to."

Deacon shook his head. "First of all, they're not people. They're monsters. But secondly, I wasn't aware that Hence made it a habit to pass through someone entirely."

This time his granddaughter shook her head. "He doesn't, as far as I know. Not his entire body. But his hands, his feet, that sword of his." She returned to her seat and slumped in the chair. "If those . . . monsters feel just a fraction of the pain and loss I felt . . . it almost makes me feel sorry for them."

Deacon placed his hands on the desk. "Pain and loss. You know Hence's background and how he became what he is."

"Painfully aware. Now. I wouldn't say I felt his, I guess, memories. Not directly. But when his form left mine, I felt like a bit of my own being was pulled out with him."

Deacon did not like the sound of that, and it was something they would need to investigate later. For now, there were more pressing matters. He reached for his granddaughter's hand across the desk. "How are you feeling now?

She let him took her hand and squeeze it reassuringly. Abigail smiled. "I can go on. Nothing feels missing now. Nothing different."

Hence cleared his throat from the doorway. "Our guest is snoring."

Abigail pulled her hand away as Hence entered the office and took the remaining chair next to her.

Hence was wearing the same clothing he wore earlier today, and yesterday, and every other day since he joined Solemn Judgment. Deacon took measure of the man before speaking. Hence was a teammate, and a valuable one, but if he hurt his granddaughter in anyway . . .

He put that thought aside. "Abigail told me what happened."

Hence ignored him and looked directly at Abigail instead. "Are you okay?"

Abigail nodded. "Yes, I think so."

Deacon watched as Hence reached out to her to place a hand on his granddaughter's shoulder. The man stopped short when he caught Deacon's gaze.

Hence slowly pulled his hand back. "I am sorry. I don't know what happened, but I am sorry."

She slowly nodded.

Hence continued. "And it won't happen again."

She finally looked at him. "Okay."

A tense air filled the room. Deacon broke it by retrieving a computer tablet from a desk drawer. "Like I told Abigail, I was watching a few feeds online, so I know the basics of what happened. I'll need you to jot down some specifics about the events inside the building. Assuming he's the one that created that construct that attacked the two of you – "

"The three of us." Abigail let the slightest smile dance across her face. "Voodoo Cowboy was there, too."

Deacon conceded. "You're right. The three of you."

Abigail nodded.

Hence was better at keeping a straight face.

Deacon continued. "Did either of you recognize that man?"

They both shook their head.

"I didn't recognize him either, so I sent a screenshot to our friends in Seattle. If the Professionals don't recognize him, they have the tech to run his face through . . . whatever it is they're able to do." Deacon could use a computer, and was quite good at it. He had no problem with his tablet, his iPad, and even though they hardly used it anymore, he was still rather adept at programming their VCR. But he didn't like to have any of his systems connected to the computers in DC or even their Service Region Office. Abigail had to be listed and registered to operate in the field, but the more he could keep her off the Protocols' radar, the better.

Hence straightened and reached across the desk. "I didn't recognize him, but I might have recognized something he was carrying. Can I see the video?"

Deacon handed him the tablet, and watched as Hence focused to become solid enough to interact with the electronics. Deacon turned his attention back to his granddaughter while Hence squinted and let his fingers scan through the video.

"What can you tell me about our guest?"

Abigail shook her head. "Not much. When we got inside the building, there were these . . . monsters. Unnaturally large, red skin."

"Horned?"

Abigail corrected her grandfather. "No. Our guest is the only one with horns or even those pointed ears. Also, his eyes were different."

"How?"

"The ones that fought us didn't have eyes. Or, not normal eyes. Where their eyes should have been were just blank pits of fire. Our guest's eyes looked normal. Oh, and he still has hair."

Before Deacon could ask another question, Hence interrupted them. "Got it." He handed the tablet back. "That box. It's a canopic chest."

Abigail looked confused. Deacon let Hence further explain.

"I should have recognized it right away, but I thought you were pulling my leg about sending us to the Blackstone with those fake Egyptain sculptures above the door."

Deacon spread his hands. "I assure you, I wasn't."

Hence continued. "I know. Anyway. That box. It's a canopic chest, and I'm betting there are still some canopic jars in it."

"You know this how? And what is a canopic jar?"

"I was . . . I used to be an archaeologist, Abigail. The ancient Egyptians used them during the mummification process. The removed the organs of the deceased and stored them in jars to bury them with the body. There would usually be four of them, and sometimes they were all kept in a box or a chest."

His jaw tightened. "I should have recognized the markings on it right away. I've been away from my studies for a long time."

"You were all distracted keeping people safe." Deacon set the tablet aside before standing. "I may ask for your help later, Hence, investigating that. But we have a house guest we need to deal with, and I don't know how long Abigail's magical barriers will keep him in his room."

Before Abigail could protest, he raised a hand. "That's not a slight on you, granddaughter. We're just dealing with an unknown. And the unknown can be dangerous."

CHAPTER 9

Four hours, forty-night minutes since the explosion . . .

Art's head throbbed, and his joints throbbed along with it. Fiery bolts of pain raced from the top of his scalp, down his spine and into his legs, and back again. His hands and fingers felt stiff, and his wrists fought him as he tried to rotate them to push feeling back into his extremities. His feet and ankles gave him the same fight.

And that was before he opened his eyes.

His eyelids dragged themselves across his aching eyeballs. He knew he was lying on his back, and he didn't feel like he was outside, so it made sense he would see some sort of ceiling above him. That didn't surprise him.

What did surprise him were the pair of hands now hovering in front of his face. Absurdly red and large muscled hands. Hands that reacted when he tried to open and close his own hands.

Were these his hands? How could these be his own hands?

Then he remembered the last time he saw these hands, the last time he saw his hands. They were holding a pickaxe and he . . .

Art sat up. The scorching song ringing in his head floated to the back of his brain, and he almost fell back down. Steadying himself by placing his hands behind him, he realized he was lying on a bed. No. Sitting on bed with a dark gray weighted blanket covering his waist and legs.

Noticing the blanket meant noticing his own bare waist and stomach. He didn't look right. He didn't feel right.

He killed someone. He used that pickaxe and killed someone. Art leaned forward and held his head in his hands.

And took them away when his thick fingers brushed against something ridged and rough that seemed to be connected to, no, growing out of his head. He brought his hands down, but not before they moved across his ears and finding they now felt taller, longer, and pointed.

The room seemed to wobble as he jumped to his feet. The blanket fell away revealing his nakedness, but he didn't spend time focusing on that. He just wanted to know where he was, and how to get home.

But Blackstone Hall wasn't safe. Something in the back of his heated brain murmured to him that he couldn't go back there.

There was death there.

And not just the death he caused.

His ears hurt, and he was reminded again that something had been done to them. Something had been done to him.

What happened? How did he get here? Where was here?

Art tried to steady his breathing to take stock of his surroundings. He was in a bedroom. There was the bed, a dresser, a chair . . . and that was all. The room was bare otherwise. There wasn't even a mirror.

But he did see the door. He moved toward it, his large bare feet bringing him to it quickly. With a thick muscular hand, he grabbed the door knob and twisted.

It didn't move.

He pulled.

It refused to budge.

He pulled harder, feeling the strange new muscles in his back and arms tighten and strain.

The doorknob came off in his hand.

Letting the now-misshapen doorknob fall to the floor, Art stepped back. If his body was now suddenly this new shape, he decided to use it and rushed the door. His shoulder slammed into it, shaking it and rattling the door frame. He heard wood crack and walls bend.

But the door still stood.

He took a few more steps back and tried again. And again.

The door never opened. It bent more than it should, but after every shoulder-ramming attempt, Art was blocked.

He was trapped.

Art turned his back to the door and surveyed the room again. There was the bed, the chair, the dresser. What now occurred to him was what this room was missing. No closet. No windows. No mirror.

He yanked open the top dresser drawer, and found it empty. He pulled it out and tossed it behind him before opening the second drawer. It was empty as well. The third and final drawer also contained nothing.

Art stood there, in front of the dresser, naked, angry, confused, defeated. Again, he asked himself what had happened. He tried to remember anything other than hitting someone in the skull with a pickaxe. What happened before that? Why did he have a pickaxe? Who did he kill?

Footsteps. He could hear footsteps. Outside the unmoving door, he could make out approaching footsteps. At least two pairs of them.

Art looked around the room again, looking for something to use as a weapon to defend himself. There was still nothing other than the basic furniture.

So that's what he used.

He shouldn't have been able to pick up the heavy wooden dresser like he did, but it felt so light and so delicate in his hands. Like the dresser drawers. Like the doorknob. Art was so much stronger than before.

He tried to hold the dresser over his head, but with his new height, he couldn't without touching the ceiling. Holding it to the side then, he moved beside the door, and watched.

Light from the other side of the door was visible through the hole where the doorknob used to be. And then something blocked it as the sound of the footsteps stopped. Art strained his newly-pointed ears and tried to listen. Someone on the other side of the door said something he couldn't understand, there was a buzzing sound, and then the door deliberately opened inward

Art waited for whoever it was to enter the room. A man in a light brown button-up jacket stepped through the doorway.

He swung the dresser like an oversized club.

The dresser passed through the man like he wasn't really there.

But he was there, and he did react. He looked at Art, held up his hands, and . . . softly smiled. "Whoa. It's okay. You're safe."

Art didn't feel safe and swung again.

The dresser passed through the man a second time, and smashed against the doorframe. Art let its pieces fall out of his hand as he took a step back.

The man held both of his hands up. "Can you understand me?"

Art looked past him and saw two others moving behind him – a woman with red hair and a much older gentleman. Were they really there, or would he pass through them, too?

He knew there was only one way to find out.

Art charged.

The man with his hands held up made a face as Art ran through him. Art felt something tug at him, holding him, but he pushed on.

The man gasped, and Art was released to plow through to the woman.

He knocked her back and with a sweep of his beefy arm, pushing her aside. Art yelled as he moved past her and continued to the older man.

He lifted a fist to knock his remaining captor to the floor.

"You will stop!" The woman was pushing herself against a wall to stand. She sought Art's eyes with her own, and locked on to them. Her eyes flickered like a just-lit candle.

Art tried to swing, but his fist was held fast in the air. A green bubble of light grew around it, holding it in place. Art tried to push through it, past it. The bubble wavered, and allowed him just a few inches of movement.

The old man had taken several steps back. The woman placed herself between him and Art, and continued to glare at him, her features set into a firm scowl. She grit her teeth and without opening her clenched jaws, she continued to yell at him.

"Stop! Now!"

Art pushed forward, but it was getting harder and harder to do so. He felt his strength leaving him. His ears rang. His entire skull felt like it was on fire.

The woman brought her own hand up in front of her face and made a sort of flicking movement with her fingers at him. He felt a wave of cool force smack him in the face.

And then he was on his back.

Art realized he could not move as the there-but-not-really-there man he hit with the dresser stepped over him. He looked down at Art.

"You're safe." He pointed at the woman with his thumb. "It might not seem like it, but Abby here isn't trying to hurt you. If she lets you stand, will you go back to your room? Sit down so we can talk?"

Art tried to move his head back and forth, looking at the man to the woman and back again, but his neck was frozen. A wave of panic rushed through his chest, but he fought against it with several steady breaths. He didn't know what was happening to him.

The woman looked familiar. So did the man. They were at Blackstone Hall. The man had some sort of weird sword, and the woman . . . what kind of power was that? Art remembered his Aunt Delphia. She used to be able to do things like this woman was doing. She was . . .

The panic was subsiding and replaced with realization. His aunt.

Aunt Delphy. She used to be a hero. Before she was hurt. That was years ago. But Art remembered the stories and the pictures.

That was years before he himself was hurt. He hurt now, but not in the same way. There was a dull ache in his leg, but it was overridden by the ringing in his head and the angry cramps in his back and shoulders. Something felt like it was trying to crawl out of the base of his spine. And his head thrum-thrum-thrummed to the beat of an angry heart.

He felt the panic again, but slowed his breathing even more and closed his eyes.

After several breaths, Art opened them. He still couldn't move, but if he could, he would have nodded.

The there-not-there man seemed to guessed that, and extended his hand to Art. "Abby will let you go now."

And the green bubbles around his fists — at some point she must have done something to his other hand — blinked away. Art tried to lift his head, and he found he could move again.

He took the man's hand. This time, the there-not-there man was solid.

Art returned to sitting on the bed, listening to the older man in the chair across from him. Brief introductions were made before the there-not-there man — Hence Williams — left to leave the woman — Abigail — standing in the doorway while her grandfather — Deacon — addressed him.

"I'm told you helped my granddaughter. Maybe even saved her." Deacon offered a soft smile. "Thank you for that."

Art nodded.

Deacon continued. "Do you remember what happened?"

Art's tongue felt heavy as he answered. "Only some." His voice didn't sound right to him. It was deep and frizzled.

"What do you remember? Do you remember who you are?"

Art nodded again. "I'm a student at PSU. Arturo Banks."

When Art said his name, Deacon looked to his granddaughter. "Get Hence on that."

Abigail shot a concerned look at Art before looking back to her grandfather. "Now?"

"Now." Deacon levelled his gaze at Art. "Mr. Banks and I will be fine."

Art didn't want to hurt anybody. Not anybody else. Not now.

These people might be able to help him. He looked at Abigail and tried to smile. His lips felt cracked and ropey.

He thought he heard Abigail sigh as she left the doorway.

And then they were alone.

Art started to speak, but Deacon held up his hand. "No. Let me speak first." Deacon leaned back in the chair before taking a deep breath. "We'll do our best to find out what happened to you, Mr. Banks. But we're going to need you to help us, too."

"How?"

"We need to know what happened to you as much as you do. We need to know what happened at Blackstone Hall."

Art felt the pounding in his head burning behind his eyes. He tried to think back to the Blackstone, to what happened to him, to what happened to the other students.

He assumed he knew the answer, but he asked anyway. "Did anyone else survive?"

Deacon shook his head. "None that have been reported."

Art looked away.

Deacon continued. "The authorities have pulled several bodies from the wreckage. There will be an investigation, of course, but my granddaughter told me what she and Hence saw." He leaned forward. "They saw more beings like you."

Art reached up and touched his right ear. "Like me?"

"Well, almost like you. She described beings almost as large as you, but they didn't have any hair."

Art remembered the person he brained with the pickaxe having had no hair, and swallowed hard. "What were they?"

Deacon shook his head. "That's what we're hoping to find out, Mr. Banks."

Art watched as Deacon stood. The older man with the stark white hair paced the width of the room. "Do you remember anyone else there? Other students? Other people?"

Art squeezed his eyes shut and held the bridge of his nose. There were others. The other students. Not all of them were exposed to whatever . . .

"Father Override. He did something to them."

Deacon paused and crossed the room again. "Father Override. We'll look into that name." He settled back in the chair. "Do you remember anyone else?"

And Art did. At first, the memories of the day were distorted, like he was looking at them through thick black smoke. Then the smoke cleared, but now he watched them as if he was viewing the day's events through so much heat that the image was liquid and rippling.

Then, the heat whooshed out of his brain, and remembered clearly.

He remembered everything. His friend Peter. The other students. The woman Luann/Stillborn. The man Jon/Still Life. That dancing phone. The hidden basement. The office beneath Blackstone Hall.

Art remembered everything, and relayed it all to Deacon. He couldn't talk fast enough. His tongue fought him as he forced out the words, but Deacon gave no indication he couldn't understand him.

His words only seemed to really fail him when he told Deacon about the . . . was it a portal? The portal Father Override and Stillborn forced him to stare into. He tried to explain what he saw, what he felt, when he was forced to stare into whatever that portal was showing him.

Deacon let Art fight with the words, never interrupting or rushing him. He just sat in the chair, listening.

Art felt like something had started to overtake him in the basement of Blackstone Hall. Clearly something had transformed him, but it was more than that. There was a presence invading him, another mind, another consciousness filling his brain when he stood before the portal. He couldn't look away. He couldn't pull away.

Art's shoulders slumped as he told Deacon the rest of what he remembered. He recounted the explosion happening in front of him, the students that hadn't been transformed catching fire and burning. Luann and Jon taking refuge behind Father Override while the fire destroyed the students' bodies as they just stood there, motionless, letting the fire consume them.

"The explosion knocked me back, and I think I was knocked out." Art looked away from Deacon and at the ceiling. "When I came to, I heard the fighting. I was drawn to it."

Deacon waited until Art made it clear he wasn't going to continued. "And that's when you helped my granddaughter."

Art nodded. "But after that, I don't remember anything else."

"That's all right. You've remembered a lot, and I am truly sorry I asked you relive it again." Deacon stood and walked to the doorway.

Art realized Abigail had been standing there, also listening. How long had she been there? Did it really matter?

Abigail held a folded blanket in her arms. She entered the room and handed it to Art. "Here. I'm sorry we don't have any clothes in your size."

The remembered realization that he'd been telling his story to Deacon and his granddaughter while naked flushed across his face. He didn't think either of them would have noticed. No doubt his face was as red as the rest of his body.

He unfolded it and draped it over his lap.

"Are you hungry?" Abigail waited until Art was covered. "Hence won't be joining us, but Grandfather and I haven't eaten yet."

"I don't know if I'm hungry or not. Nothing feels right to me right now. I don't even know what I look like."

Abigail nodded. "You look different than you did before, unless you had horns and a devil tail when you woke up this morning."

Deacon shot her a look. "Really, Abigail?"

She shrugged. "Stating the obvious, Grandfather." Abigail looked at Art. "Would you like to see what you look like?"

Art nodded.

Abigail lifted both hands in front of her chest, her palms facing outward. She licked her upper lip, and made a noise with her mouth he could only describe as shiny.

A shimmering rectangle of light formed on her outward facing palms. It grew a few feet high and a few less feet wide. Its surface shimmered, glowed silver, then slowly calmed into a mirrored surface.

It was a reflection of him sitting on the bed, the blanket covering his waist and legs, leaving his massive chest and shoulders exposed. His deep red skin seemed to strain to contain the muscles underneath. He moved his hands and arms, confirming this reflection was truly him.

Art reached for his head. His ears were exaggeratingly long and pointed, and just behind his ears were ridged horns pointing straight up to the ceiling. He gingerly touched them. They were rough, and definitely felt connected to him. The base of his horns disappeared in his hair somewhere, but his fingers found where they connected to his scalp. The skin was ragged and felt raw where they sprouted from his skull.

As he was examining his head, a red tail with a clubbed tip slunk around from his back to his front.

Art looked away. "I don't want to see anymore."

Abigail dropped her hands, and the magic mirror immediately evaporated.

Deacon stood. "We will determine what happened to you, Mr. Banks." He reached for Art's hand. "But, first, will you join us for dinner?"

CHAPTER 10

Hence Williams didn't need to join them for dinner. He didn't need to eat. He hadn't needed to eat since that night in Egypt, so while the others had their meal, he returned to Deacon's office, took the main tablet, and retreated to his own room down the hall.

Hence's bedroom was a bedroom in name only. He didn't have a bed. He didn't need one. Not because he didn't want to sleep or even that he couldn't sleep. He just didn't need to need to sleep.

Instead of a bed, the room was occupied by Hence's desk, shelves of books, and a computer with an older-style mechanical keyboard. He found it easier to use this style of keyboard when focusing on his fingers and forcing them to become solid. He also preferred the sound it made when he used it. It reminded him of the old Remington typewriter he used before his misadventures in Egypt so many years ago.

Other mementos of his life from that time filled the room. Framed photographs decorated the walls, highlighting his time as an Egyptologist and even before. Places he'd been that no longer exist as they did during that time. Friends and colleagues long deceased. One photo was of him and his family before he left America the first time. He sometimes wondered what his younger sister Arabella would think of what became of his life, or, specifically, his existence. She loved reading the stories in "The Argosy" or "The Blue Book," much to their mother's dismay. Hence often thought his existence sometimes resembled those found in those old 15-cent magazines, and more times than he could remember, he found himself wishing she was still alive so he could share stories of his adventures with her.

Beneath a photo of his sister when she was eight-years-old was a framed New York newspaper from 1923. It was the newspaper announcing his disappearance and assumed death. He didn't need a reminder of that incident, but Deacon thought it would be helpful to have a physical and tangible reminder of what his life was before what happened to him.

As for Abigail, she thought it would be helpful to give him a model of the Great Pyramid at one point several years ago, and it sat completed on his desk next to his monitor. She was right. Building and painting that model did help him learn how best to make his hands and fingers solid enough to manipulate small objects. He couldn't remember if he ever properly thanked her.

Hence focused and grabbed the mouse. He had a long time since Egypt to learn how emerging technologies worked, and that extended to being able to use a computer.

It only took him a few minutes to find anything online about their guest. Arturo Banks was a second-year student at Portland State University. He came to PSU on a football scholarship last year, but after a career-ending injury, that scholarship was taken away. However, he managed to find enough financial aid elsewhere to stay in school. He was studying Applied Health and Fitness, and after Hence hopped through a few electronic hoops, he was able to learn that the kid was doing okay grade-wise.

Hence expanded his online search, searching for information about Banks before he started attending Portland State. He found that Banks was born to large family in Carthage, Texas, but before Hence could dig any deeper than that, Deacon's tablet buzzed.

Someone was calling it.

Hence used some books from the nearest bookshelf to prop the tablet on his desk. He made sure his fingers were solid enough before delicately pressing the button to accept the incoming call.

He knew from the name on the screen that someone from the Professionals was calling. Hence didn't know who it would be, though.

He didn't expect it to be Michelle Barnes, the Professional also known as Blindspot. She wasn't in her too-bright white unitard uniform, but rather a loose t-shirt and scarf. Her civilian clothes really made her grey eyes stand out. She wore her blonde hair loose around her shoulders. She sipped from a tall cup of coffee, and was in mid-swallow when Hence picked up the call.

Michelle set the cup aside. "Deacon called Mike?"

Hence smiled. "You're not Mike."

"And you're not Deacon." Michelle returned a tired grin. "Manhandle's not here. He took a few days off. He's actually probably closer to you than me right now."

"Oh?"

She rolled her gray eyes. "He's in Astoria with Chet."

"Chet?"

"Sorry. Undertow. He's back out and . . . " She let her voice trail off and interrupted the awkwardness in her voice with another sip of her coffee. As she was about to speak again, Hence heard someone on her side of their communication calling for her in the background.

Hence raised an eyebrow. "Do you need to take that?"

Michelle turned back to whoever was calling her and raised her voice to make a point. "She'll be fine." She turned back to face Hence. "Deacon sent some images he needed help with?"

Hence nodded. "We're working on something, and was hoping you Professionals could lend a hand."

"Why didn't Deacon just call someone at the DC office?"

"He trusts Mike more than anyone at the Protocols."

This time Michelle raised an eyebrow. "I have friends there. Rothchild can be trusted."

"I'm sure he can be. For now, though, he thought Mike could help."

"Well, like I said, Mike isn't here." She smiled again. "So you'll have to settle for me."

Hence didn't spend a lot of time working with other teams or aug-humans. With the exception of Voodoo Cowboy, this particular phase of Hence's life and career had been spent exclusively with Solemn Judgment. Solemn Judgment occasionally teamed with other heroes but even then, Hence preferred to stay in the background. He wasn't even sure if Michelle/Blindspot or Mike/Manhandle or even Troy/Voodoo Cowboy for that matter really knew how old he was or what happened to him in the first place. It wasn't that he was trying to hide who he was. After many conversations with Deacon, they both just thought it was best that the fewer people who knew how old Hence Williams was, the better.

Politically, it made sense, too. He didn't know if the statute of limitations had run out at this point, but he wasn't sure how the current Egyptian government would react to his unlicensed excavations in their country the 1920s. It meant not being 100% truthful with the Nixon Protocols registration requirements, but no one on Solemn Judgment wanted to give the United States government any reason to turn Hence Williams over to another nation's law enforcement agencies.

"Well?" Michelle was staring at him through the screen.

He shook his head and refocused. "Sorry. There's a lot going on here right now."

"We noticed. You made the news."

He sighed. "We thought we might. Deacon was monitoring that, but no one's said anything about the man with the canopic chest."

"The what?"

"The box. Deacon was hoping your computer systems might be able to identify to man holding it."

She nodded. "We got a hit in our system. I'll send you what we have. It's not as in depth as what you might have gotten from DC, though" She paused and seemed to choose her next words carefully. "Your team is at least filing this the Service Region Office, right?"

Hence was quick to respond. "Of course."

Michelle slowly nodded. "Right."

She probably didn't mean to sound like she was questioning him, but Hence still didn't like the sound of her response. "You can ask Rothchild. Deacon is always on top of the paperwork." And then he didn't like his own response, realizing he was sounding overly defensive. "Solemn Judgment follows all the rules, but the folks in DC don't always understand the kinds of things we deal with."

That seemed to placate her. "You're not wrong. Even with Rothchild out there, they have a hard time with the stranger cases we work sometimes." That same person who called for Michelle earlier called for her again. "Give me a moment and I'll get what we have sent to you." A woman with purple skin wearing a navy blue jumpsuit appeared behind Michelle. Hence couldn't see her face, and he didn't recognize the outfit. He couldn't think of anyone with purple skin currently on the Professionals team. Whoever it was, she said something Hence didn't quite catch, but Michelle must have.

Michelle gave Hence a final smile. "Tell Abigail I said, 'Hello.'" And then the connection was dropped.

Almost immediately after the call ended, Deacon's tablet lit up with an incoming message notification from the Professionals. Hence opened it and scanned the information before standing and heading for the dining room.

CHAPTER 11

James Lappeus, the man now known as Father Override, sat alone in the main office of the Goldendale Observatory. His hounds – Luann and Jon Heckler – had been sent away to run errands, gather equipment or people, and basically just leave him alone. They were loyal Hounds, and served him as well as they could. James tried to appreciate that as he was losing his patience when things didn't go as expected.

Solemn Judgment's appearance at Blackstone Hall was one of those unexpected things.

He may have snapped at Luann for, how did that one actor put it all those years ago when James owned the Oro Fino Theater . . . going off script. He'd make a point of consoling her in the morning before going after the giant's heart. He would have to make her understand the amount of pressure he was under, and having some so-called heroes like Solemn Judgment become aware of his activities had the potential of interfering with his deadline.

He pinched his nose between his eyes and squeezed. He felt a headache coming.

It was one of *those* headaches.

And it meant Chambreau wanted to speak with him.

James rose from his seat and made for the South Dome. He owed Chambreau everything, a fact that the man never let him forget every time they communicated with one another.

Perhaps calling him a man now was inaccurate. When James first met Edouard Chambreau, he was a ruthless, conniving swindler whose humanity could be judged only by the fact that he was ambitious, driven, and walked around on two legs. Chambreau was always someone who relentlessly pursued wealth, power, and control, and he never seemed to care who got in his way in pursuit of these goals.

Chambreau brought him into his line of work, making James Lappeus a Hound in the 1840s. While they were involved in a number of schemes that fleeced the San Francisco gold miners of their earnings, it wasn't until years later in Oregon when Chambreau reentered his life and made him an offer for something more than stolen winnings at a Faro table.

He wasn't cheating at cards anymore. Edouard Chambreau was cheating at life.

The Hounds were run out of California in 1849, and James found himself setting up shop in Portland running the Oro Fino Theater and Gem Saloon. He was good at it. James made honest money in addition to what he was able to take through other less-than-legal activities.

Chambreau made him realize, though, this was not enough. Not for people like Chambreau, and not for people like him. And when he made him a Hound again, this time it wasn't just a name used to scare the community. This time, being a Hound came with power.

Real power. Power to corrupt. Power to control. Power to make others better and, in doing so, making them indebted to him.

But in receiving that power, James Lappeus was now indebted tp Chambreau.

What Chambreau had become between the time he was run out of San Francisco with James and now, James could not understand. And it didn't matter. He owed Chambreau his service, not out of friendship or any other warm feelings, but out of obligation.

James would not have had his law enforcement career if not for Chambreau. Someone else would have been named Chief of Police. Someone else would have been put in a position to help Chambreau by making sure his illegal saloon activities were ignored by the authorities.

And when Chambreau began having him arrest the women praying outside his establishment, James knew it wasn't just because the women were disturbing the peace when all they were doing was protesting the sale of liquor.

James entered the South Dome and looked up at the main telescope. The headache was starting to subside, but if he didn't reach out to Chambreau soon he knew it would get far worse.

Metal loudly squirming against the hard floor filled the dome as James ascended the metal steps of the rolling ladder to the telescope's eyepiece.

When they took over the Goldendale Observatory last week, the first thing James had his Hounds do was change the coordinates of the telescope. The exact coordinates were given to him in a vision from Edouard Chambreau. Luann questioned it, of course. Jon never faltered and always followed his instructions, but the sister challenged him.

When she asked about what they were supposed to be looking at in the telescope, James couldn't give her an answer. He sent her away to make sure the employees of the Observatory were turned into her Born Again subjects. They were to have no interruptions while they occupied the building, so the staff were made to contact their friends and family on a semi-regular basis to keep anyone from questioning why the Observatory demanded so much of their time. Visiting hours were cut off. Communication with the outside world was limited to the bare minimum to keep anyone from asking questions.

While James kept Luann busy with that, he did a bit of research himself. Chambreau had instructed him to point the telescope at something designated in Goldendale's catalogs as "IC 2118."

Something broiled behind James' eyes. The headache grew stronger. He grabbed the handrail to steady himself. The room was already chilly, but as he brought his eye to the eyepiece, the temperature seemed to drop at least a dozen degrees.

But James Lappeus was only cold for a moment.

Every time he put his eye to the telescope, he didn't see stars, or space, or any planet or moon. Instead, despite the instrument being pointed to the sky, what he saw in the telescope eyepiece looked like an overhead view of the Pacific Northwest.

That image was only there for a moment, and then it went oily black. The room filled with heat. James jerked his head back to see the South Dome filled with flickering flames. Red flashes of fire curtained the rounded walls of the room. In that brief moment, he already felt beads of sweat forming on his forehead and across his face.

He didn't understand the ritual here. Why did he need to look into the eyepiece for Chambreau to come to him here? Couldn't he just look into the telescope to see into wherever Chambreau now was?

James sat down on the top steps of the ladder as the light in the room grew brighter. The red tongues of fire glowed orange, then yellow, then bright white. He held his hand to his face again. He wasn't trying to squeeze off another headache.

He was just protecting his eyes. His friend may have granted him extraordinary powers, but protected eyesight wasn't one of them.

The room dimmed. James lowered his hand and cautiously looked around the room.

Standing in as close to the middle of the dome as possible was his old friend Edouard Chambreau.

He was still his old friend, wasn't he? Clearly, he'd changed since their time in San Francisco, or even since they worked together in Portland. Physically, he still looked like Edouard. Rugged. A thick, dark steel wool beard streaked gray. A face worn by the elements. Eyes beaded behind heavy eyelids.

But there was a fire behind those eyes.

The temperature of the room returned to normal, which James realized was perhaps the only normal thing about the South Dome at the moment. Two men that should have been long dead looked at each other.

And the one standing in the near-center of the room began laughing.

James stood and descended the stepladder. Chambreau's laughter trailed off as he opened his arms toward James. James hesitated as he noticed what Chambreau was wearing – something that looked like a cartoonish version of a Native American's scouting outfit.

Chambreau noticed James' hesitation. "Ne vous laissez pas surprendre par mon apparence." Even Chambreau's voice sound as it should, but somehow different, the French accent thicker than it was the last time they spoke. Chambreau grinned and switched to English. "Let me change my appearance."

James' vision wavered for less than a second, like he was walking through a heated room and the lines of everything flickered. And then Chambreau was wearing a dark brown suit. His beard was shaped, and his dark brown hair was slicked back.

"My apologies, James. I had other business before meeting with you." His turned his head from side to side, flicking his eyes at his still open arms. "Come to me, James."

James stepped forward and accepted the embrace.

Chambreau's arms were cold, his skin icy. He smelled overly sweet, like he was wearing something to mask his real scent. James didn't breath in too deeply, but he was able to pick up a rotten farm smell beneath it.

After a moment, Chambreau released him. He stared at James, into James, and lowered his voice.

"Racontez-moi votre progression." Chambreau's accent wasn't as thick now, but he still slipped between French and English. "Do you have it?"

James nodded. "We do."

"Les viscères. Where are you keeping it?"

"The viscera? It's safe. We have it protected."

James watched Chambreau as he took several small steps around the room, seeming to consider what he had been told.

Finally, he stopped pacing and looked back at James. "Très bien. Good. And the heart of the giant?"

James nodded. "Tomorrow. We'll have it tomorrow."

Chambreau rubbed his hands together. His palms sounded like thick sandpiper against dense wood. "And the skull? L'enfant?"

"You'll have it. I've had to make some changes to our timetable."

Chambreau's face darkened and he let his hands fall to his sides. "Why?"

"We've attracted some unwanted attention."

"From who? Dis m'en plus?"

"There's a group of . . . heroes."

"Heroes? Des justiciers?"

The switching between languages was beginning to wear on James' ears. The way the non-English words slid out of Chambreau's mouth made James half-expect to see a slime trail across his cheeks.

He made an effort not to focus on that. "Heroes. They were there when we retrieved the box."

"But they did not stop you, non?"

"Stop us? No."

"What are you not telling me, James?"

James could not meet Chambreau's eyes. "My control over the Hounds is slipping. Luann gets . . . distracted."

"And her brother does not keep her on track?"

"I'm sure having him there helps."

That was true. Jon did help to keep Luann more focused. She was less likely to forget her immediate goals if he was there to remind her of her duties. And maybe if they had been able to keep the possessed Born Again, tomorrow's tasks would not be as difficult, especially now that Solemn Judgment was aware of their activities.

But was it Luann's activities that brought Solemn Judgment there in the first place?

James scratched at this beard. He didn't know.

"What is it, James?"

"This group of heroes calls themselves Solemn Judgment. They

aren't like the normal law enforcement. They tend to focus on . . . "
He took a deep breath. "I made a point of learning about the locals
when we set up camp here in Goldendale. I thought since we're in
Washington, we'd have a different group to worry about. But this
Solemn Judgment . . . they tend to focus on situations of an occult
nature."

Chambreau's eyes narrowed, appearing to consider what James
just told him. James waited for a response.

He didn't expect another laugh.

"James, my friend. Ne sois pas ridicule! This is foolish. It does not
matter."

"It . . . doesn't?"

"Of course not." Chambreau clapped his hands together. "Laisse
tomber."

"Drop it? When we were run out of San Francisco – "

"You came back stronger!" Chambreau's eyes flashed white. "You
had no business surviving that and becoming more powerful in
Oregon. And you have more power now than we did then." He
lowered his voice. "You don't deserve it, but you have power. Do you
not have enough power now, James? Did I not give you enough?"

James' back and shoulders stiffened. "Of course you gave me a
enough."

Did Chambreau just smile. "Good. Then tomorrow you shall get
me the heart. And the skull?"

"Tomorrow as well."

Chambreau slowly nodded. "Good."

"I still don't understand why you want – "

The room flashed hot again, and then James Lappeus was alone
again in the South Dome.

CHAPTER 12

Eighteen hours, twelve minutes since the explosion . . .

Arturo Banks' heart pounded away in his chest, threatening to break free. He woke with a start, cramps rippling through his body. His hands shook, and when he touched his face, they shook harder. His ears were different.

No. They were like this last night, long and pointed.

His fingers pushed through his thick hair until he found where the horns erupted from his scalp.

He yanked his hands away and sat up, flinging the blanket aside. He was naked. He remembered not having any clothes here.

Here. Where was here? What happened last night?

Slowly, his thoughts settled. He focused on his heartbeat the way that older man Mr. Williams tried to teach him last night. The hammering in his heavily-muscled chest slowed.

Art swung his legs over the side of the bed, and as much as he wanted the events of yesterday to be a dream, as he looked down at his feet and legs with their red skin and corded muscle, he had to accept that yesterday wasn't a dream.

It might have been a nightmare.

And he hadn't woken up yet.

He started to remember. Yesterday, he was in this room. He woke up here before. Art was naked then, too, but yesterday there wasn't a stack of clothing in the chair opposite the bed.

There also wasn't a mirror in the room yesterday, but it seemed his host mounted one on the wall behind the chair for him.

Art studied his face for a moment before standing and approaching the mirror to give himself a full inspection. His body was very different than it was this time yesterday. Whatever happened to him at Blackstone Hall did not "wear off" as one of his hosts – the there-not-there man named Mr. Williams – had suggested might happen. Mr. Andrews didn't seem to think that was a possibility.

And he was right. If nothing, Art's body felt more normal today than it did last night. He watched himself in the mirror, flexing muscles and even causing his new tail to flick and flail around behind him. Art turned around and tried to look over his shoulder to see what he looked like from behind. That tail grew out of the base of his spine, and he found it surprisingly easy to command the muscles controlling it to move.

He reached for the clothes laid out for him. As he put on the gray sweatpants and white t-shirt, he thought back to last night, remembering what he could and filling in the blanks with what the others told him.

There was a fight at Blackstone Hall. An explosion. A minor gas leak blew out the just-discovered basement and most of the first floor, but the building still stood. A man name Jon and his sister Luann arrived at the Blackstone at some point before he got out of class. He learned the name of the man the same time the older gentleman and the granddaughter Abigail did. Mr. Williams showed Deacon a tablet, and apparently there was an email from, of all things, a superhero team in Seattle. The Professionals. Art had heard of them before, but this other team he'd fallen in with? He'd never heard of them before.

Solemn Judgment.

Apparently, Solemn Judgment was a team of sorts as well, although he only counted two of them, three if he included Mr. Andrews in that count. Art didn't get the impression Mr. Andrews left his home much, though.

Mr. Andrews read the email and announced the name of the man Art had seen in the basement of Blackstone Hall was Jon Heckler. Abigail and Mr. Williams both had a chuckle at the last name. Mr. Andrews didn't waste any time, though, in looking something else up and discovering Jon had a sister named Luann. He found a picture online of Luann, and showed to Art.

Art confirmed that was the woman he first encountered in the lobby of Blackstone Hall.

Abigail and Mr. Williams explained to him what they encountered at that building. Art tried to relay what he saw and experienced, but some of his memories were still murky.

Mr. Andrews was understanding. They were all patient, and offered their home to him. Mr. Williams said he would reach out to his family in Carthage if he'd like. Art wasn't surprised they'd discovered where he was from, not after seeing that they had enough technology and contacts to discover someone's identity from just a picture. He didn't want his family to worry about him, but asked that they not be told about his new condition.

Not until he knew whether or not this could be fixed.

After the accident on the football field, Art underwent multiple surgeries, had hardware installed, removed, and reinstalled. He undertook months and months of physical therapy, and worked hard to find new financial aid that would allow him to stay enrolled in PSU after his football scholarship was understandably taken away. Art was used to hard work.

He was ready to start that work right away, even though he didn't know what that might mean. He just knew that this new body, as comfortable as it was beginning to feel, wasn't his.

Art noticed that at some point in the night, the dresser had been replaced. While he was checking the empty drawers, he noted the dresser had been bolted to the floor.

He didn't blame them.

And then he considered the closed door.

Yesterday, it was locked. Or sealed. Or somehow kept from opening for him. Abigail was some sort of magic using hero, and had done something to the door to keep him from opening it yesterday.

Was it still closed to him today?

He slowly grabbed the doorknob, remembering yesterday it came off in his hand.

The doorknob turned.

And he was able to open the door.

Art made his way to the dining room where he had eaten with the others last night. except for Mr. Williams. It was just himself with Mr. Andrews and his granddaughter. The two of them were obviously close, and Art couldn't tell if Mr. Williams' lack of presence was out of courtesy to allow the two of them a family meal, or for some other reason.

They did ask him to eat with them, however, so it must have had to do more with Mr. Williams than anything else.

A rough grumble rippled through this stomach. Art didn't realize he was hungry, but just thinking about the dining room last night reminded him he needed to eat.

Mr. Williams was in the dining room, sitting in one of the high back wooden chairs. He looked up as Art entered. "How are you feeling?"

Art noted the man was wearing the same thing he wore yesterday as he answered. "Hungry." Art's voice still sounded off, heavier, to him.

Mr. Williams nodded. "That's probably a good sign. The Andrews have never done a formal breakfast here, but there's plenty of food in the kitchen."

"What about you?"

"I'm sorry?"

"Did you have breakfast?"

An awkward smile crossed Mr. Williams' face. "I don't eat. But, please. Sit."

Art took a seat across from Mr. Williams. It was coincidentally the chair he used last night.

The man looked over Art's shoulder. "He's all yours, Abby."

Art turned his head to see the woman introduced to him as Abigail Andrews standing behind him in the doorway leading to the kitchen. Unlike Mr. Williams, her clothes were different. Instead of that dark green bodysuit with the straps that looked like an upside-down star beneath her neck, she wore a loose-fitting PSU sweatshirt and matching sweatpants. Her hair was pulled back in a thick red ponytail.

She entered the dining room carrying a tray with two mugs of something hot and a platter of muffins. Abigail gestured at the cups. "It's coffee. But we have tea or juice if you'd rather."

Art reached for the coffee mug, but stopped short of touching it. It was so . . . small compared to his hand. It looked like a toy.

Abigail took the mug and offered it to him. "Go ahead."

He took it, and guzzled the hot coffee in just a few swallows.

Mr. Williams chuckled. "Looks like you'll need some bigger coffee cups."

Art made a point to gently place the mug on the table. "Thank you. That was really good."

Abigail smiled. "It's Grandfather's special blend." She sat down to join the two men. "I've already eaten, so please." She motioned at the muffins.

Art tried not to notice how miniature they appeared in his hands as he popped one after the other into his mouth.

Four muffins later, he realized the other two were looking at him. "What?"

Mr. Williams brushed the corner of his mouth with his thumb.

"You've got something . . . "

Art felt himself flush, but he didn't know if anyone noticed his red cheeks getting any redder.

"Grandfather and I were up late last night discussing you, Mr. Banks."

Art shook his head. "Art. Call me Art."

"Sorry. Art. You said that last night. Art." She took a muffin for herself and picked a bit off the top. "You're welcome to stay with us as long as you'd like. Hence spoke to your father, and assured him you're all right."

"You talked to my dad?"

Mr. Williams raised his hands. "I only told him you're okay. That's all. I didn't tell him about – "

Abigail finished eating her bit of muffin and lifted her own hand. "He doesn't know. As far as we can tell, only the three of us here and Grandfather know."

"And the people who did this to me." He felt his tail involuntarily thwack itself against the back of his chair.

"Of course. And Hence and Grandfather did some digging last night after you went to bed."

Art looked at Mr. Williams. "And?"

"The Heckler siblings should be locked up."

"For what they did to me?"

"No. They should be there now. Airway Heights in Spokane."

Art felt his hands balling into fists. "But they were here in Portland yesterday."

Abigail reached for Art and placed a cooling hand on Art's upper arm. "We know. And we're not in Portland."

"What?"

"I'm sorry. It didn't come up last night. We're in Salem."

"Salem . . . in Connecticut? With the witches." He felt his face flush again. "No offense. I mean, if you're a – "

"It's okay. And you're thinking Massachusetts. Not that Salem. Salem, Oregon. Not that far from Portland."

Art let out a calming breath.

Abigail didn't remove her hand and made a point of meeting Art's eyes. "Are you okay?"

Art slowly nodded.

Abigail nodded in return before taking her hand back and

continuing. "Last week, they were both locked up in a facility designed for aug-humans."

"Aug . . . humans?"

"Short for Augmented Humans. It's what they call us."

"They?"

"The government. Hence and I are Augmented Humans. Technically Grandfather is, too, but that's a little more complicated." She paused. "You look confused."

"I am."

"It's a lot. I know. And we'll get through all of it." She tore another bit of muffin. "But later."

Art placed his palms on the tabletop. "After you've figured out what happened to me, right? And how to get me back to normal?"

Abigail and Mr. Williams exchanged looks.

Art curled his fingers. "What?"

Abigail avoided his eyes and placed her bit of muffin down. "Since we don't know what exactly happened to you, Art, we don't know how to undo it." She reached for his arm again. "Yet. We don't know yet."

Art moved his shoulder and slid back in his chair. "I can't stay like this."

"We know you don't want to, Mr. Banks." Mr. Andrews appeared in the kitchen doorway, and unlike his granddaughter he wasn't holding a tray full of breakfast foods. Mr. Andrews carried a rolled-up map into the dining room and spread it out on the table after Abigail moved the coffee mugs and breakfast tray. "And Solemn Judgment will look into it. Right now, though, we have more pressing concerns."

More pressing concerns than . . . fixing him? Art started to stand, but the older man placated him.

"Your situation is important, Mr. Banks. But please understand, we need to be somewhere else." He looked at the others. "Now."

Abigail held down an edge of the map, keeping it from rolling up on itself. Mr. Williams stood to get a better view. Art did the same, and saw they were all looking at a map of Portland.

Mr. Andrews' fingers danced over the map, skipping through different Portland neighborhoods. Art looked at the older man's face to see him closing his eyes and gently sucking in his lips. Suddenly, Mr. Andrews' eyes snapped open, and he stabbed at the map with his forefinger.

"There." Mr. Andrews stepped back and slid into a chair. Abigail learned closer to examine the map. "That's . . . the Kenton neighborhood." She looked at the grandfather. "Are you sure?"

"The ripples are strong. And they're getting stronger. You need to go."

Mr. Williams made a fist, and a weird . . . sword appeared in his hand? Art thought it looked familiar from yesterday. The weapon with the backward curved blade glittered in Mr. Williams hand, and Art thought part of the man's body glittered for a moment as well.

Art shook his head and finally stood. He opened his mouth to speak, to question whatever was about to happen, but Mr. Andrews again cut him off.

"You should go with them, Mr. Banks."

Art felt his lips move, but the questions he had died in his throat.

"Go with them. Abigail will tell you what you need to know once you get there."

Art looked at Mr. Williams who shrugged at him. "Abby's the boss."

Mr. Andrews shook his head. "Use their codenames in the field."

Art found his voice. "Codenames? In the field? Why am I going into the field? What field?"

Abigail let the map roll away. As she brought her hands to her sides, her fingers swam through the air. Green threads of light trailed behind them. "Grandfather. Clear the table."

Mr. Andrews swept the map aside just before Abigail flung her hands at the tabletop. Those green light threads slid across the wooden surface, scraping the veneer away. As the top layer of the table dissolved, Art could see a . . . large white man with an axe?

Abigail looked to her grandfather, her eyes glowing white-green. "This is the place?"

Mr. Andrews nodded.

Abigail returned the nod before turning to her teammate. "After you?"

Mr. Williams climbed onto the edge of the table as those green light threads continued to scrub away to tabletop, further revealing a dreary day somewhere Art assumed was in Portland. The man with the axe was a statue. He could see that now. And it stood in front of a sign that in large white letters read "Historic Kenton." Art knew Kenton, or at least of Kenton, but he hadn't spent any time in that part of town. Most of his free time was spent on campus. He was normally busy with school.

Art thought he'd much rather be busy with school now. School. Classwork. Homework. Labs. Hours in the library. He missed all of that. Eating snacks from a vending machine when he needed a break. It felt like the last time he did that was years ago even though it was only yesterday. Getting up from his desk to stretch so his right leg didn't bother him as much.

His right leg didn't bother him now. It was uncomfortable, but that dull ache from the metal and surgeries wasn't there. Not now.

"Now."

Mr. Williams nodded at Abigail before taking a step into the window/opening created on the tabletop.

Art didn't want to go, and took a deliberate step away.

"I can't keep this open forever, Art." Abigail flicked another handful of light threads at the table to make the portal larger.

"I don't want to."

"Go with my granddaughter, Mr. Banks. The people that did this to you are there now. Look."

Art leaned forward, and realized this wasn't a still image. There were people there in front of that statue, some standing, some sitting.

They all had red marks and streaks at their temples.

How could Mr. Andrews know who was there? "I don't see them."

"I can tell. The brother and sister. And I'm guessing the one you described as Father Override, too. The rippling is strong and . . . angry."

Abigail nudged her chin at him. "You need to go. Once we stop them, we can find out what they did to you."

"And they'll fix me, right?" Art climbed onto the table and stepped into the opening portal. "Right?"

CHAPTER 13

To Art, it felt like stepped into a puddle without realizing how deep it was. The world splashed around him. Bright emerald streaks of light flew around his body and face. His body felt truly and entirely cool for the first time since the events at Blackstone Hall.

He felt calm.

And then he found himself standing next to a waiting Mr. Williams.

"I'm glad you came along. Here, make room for Abby."

The two of them stepped aside as Abigail Andrews materialized in front of them. She was wearing her green-and-black uniform with the gem on her chest now, and her eyes were dangerously focused on the statue in front of them.

"Don't tell her I called her that. In the field, use the names Pentacle and Revenant."

Art tried to reconcile that. "She's . . . ?"

"She's Pentacle. I'm Revenant. What should we call you?"

Art shook his head. "I . . . don't know? I'm just Art."

"That's okay. Now get ready."

Art looked over Pentacle's outfit again and then at his own clothes. He still wore the same sweatpants and t-shirt from before. He wasn't sure what he was expecting, if he was being honest with himself. Was he supposed to have some sort of costume? Mr. Williams . . . no, he said to call him Revenant. Revenant wasn't wearing anything different from before.

A woman called for him, and Art recognized her voice. "Arturo! You're alive!"

Art spotted Stillborn walking in the crowd of standing still civilians. She started toward him, pushing past her . . . what did she call them? Her Born Again. An older man with dark skin and lightning white hair wearing a tan suit, a middle-aged woman with heavy bags under her eyes and a heavier winter coat, a twenty-something in long shorts and a basketball jersey, and many others all shuffled out of their way as Stillborn approached.

She had her hands out. One of them held a scalpel.

Art brought his fists up, but Pentacle stepped in front of him. She manipulated something in front of her, but he couldn't see what with her back to him.

But he heard it. Shrack! A loud blast burst from her chest, and since he was so much taller than Pentacle, Art could see over her head to watch Stillborn fly back when a bolt of green light hit her in the face.

He couldn't help but smile when she landed on her backside and slid back several feet. Her scalpel flew from her grasp, but he lost track of it.

Pentacle advanced on her, ultimately blocking his view. Art looked around. There were so many people just standing still, only moving to turn toward Stillborn anytime she moved. Beyond the Historic Kenton sign was a bank, and he could even see people through its windows standing inside having been mesmerized by Stillborn.

And then he heard a gunshot.

He ducked, and almost laughed at himself realizing he was still a huge target even hunched over. Another gunshot rang out, and this one sounded closer. He felt a hand touch his back.

Revenant leaned closer to him. "It's okay. He's with us."

When Art finally saw the source of the gunshots, he realized he recognized the shooter. Voodoo Cowboy. Art had never seen him in person, but he was one of Portland's local semi-celebrity superheroes.

Art didn't really follow the superhero scene, not like some of his family or other students. He was too focused on his studies, especially after the football accident. But everyone on campus knew Voodoo Cowboy, and most even had a story about seeing him in action. (There was also that one girl in class that insisted she dated him once, but Art didn't think that was really true.)

And here he was now, firing guns into the crowd.

Again and again.

Art felt his shoulders tighten as he flinched with each gunshot. He glanced at Revenant. He didn't seem to mind. Pentacle was focused on Stillborn. Those Born Again were just dropping with every shot.

But aside from the marks at their temples, no one seemed to take damage from Voodoo Cowboy's barrage of gunfire. They just slid peacefully to the ground.

And did Voodoo Cowboy just make eye contact with Art? And did he just wink before turning his attention to another one of Stillborn's victims and firing a shot into their face?

Pentacle continued to block his view of Stillborn, so Art looked around for . . . he didn't know what he was looking for. Revenant was no longer at his side. Instead, the man was weaving his way through Born Again as he made his way to the bank.

What was he supposed to do?

The answer to that question presented itself when Art saw Father Override and Still Life at the base of the statue of . . . was that supposed to be Paul Bunyan?

Yes. Apparently, it was Paul Bunyan. There was a statue at least 30 feet tall in the Kenton neighborhood of Portland, Oregon. Because of course there was. Even in his short time living in the Pacific Northwest, Art had come to appreciate and even enjoy the quirks of Portland. He'd seen some of the weirder sites the town had to offer, but he'd never come out to this part of town to see the colorful concrete Paul Bunyan with the cartoony wide smile.

Father Override and Still Life were clearly here for the statue. They were at the base of it, discussing something that Art was too far away to hear.

Art's heart started beating faster, and he found himself making angry fists as he watched Father Override. That man did this to him. He forced him to stare into that portal or whatever it was. He put something inside of Art that changed him into . . . whatever this was.

He found himself yelling as he started for the statue.

Shrack! He easily passed Pentacle, and as soon as he did, he saw Stillborn. She reached for him, and when she did, all the nearby Born Again reached for him as well. Suddenly he found himself pushing through the outstretched hands of dozens of men, women, an angry-looking teenager, and somebody's grandmother in a wheelchair. They were all different, only united by the fact that they happened to be nearby when Stillborn arrived, and that they all had those wounds in the sides of their heads.

His heart pounded as he tried to push through without hurting anyone.

And then that singing started. He'd heard those off-key tones before, in Blackstone Hall when he watched his friend Peter's head open up at the temples.

He resisted the urge to clap his hands over his ears. That wouldn't stop that sound.

Getting to Father Override might, though.

He pushed through the Born Again reaching out to him. Out of the corner of his eye, he saw Pentacle throwing globs of green energy into Stillborn's face. He heard more of Voodoo Cowboy's gunshots. Behind the statue on the street, cars were pulling away, the drivers and passengers managing to escape Stillborn's powers. He thought he heard a MAX light rail train approaching its stop at the intersection in front of the bank.

That didn't matter. What mattered was Father Override.

Still Life reacted to his approach first. He turned and ran.

Father Override turned to face Art.

And opened his arms to him.

Father Override still wore that three-piece suit, but it was wrinkled. The man himself looked more disheveled than before. Circles rested beneath his eyes, and his goatee needed to be brushed.

Art moved his legs and lowered his shoulders the way he did when he was on the football field. The muscles were new but their movement felt familiar. He'd put his football aspirations behind him and was at peace with that, but Art had to admit it felt good to push his body this way. He didn't realize he could still miss this feeling.

Father Override was only a few feet away, and he was still just standing there, opening his arms to Art, smiling through his messy goatee.

Art barreled through two Born Again's arms. They fell away easily.

And then he was face-to-face with Father Override.

Art hadn't intended to stop, but something held him just inches away from his target. He strained against whatever invisible barrier Father Override had between them. The air grew hot, and the edges of Art's vision blurred red-orange as he brought his fists down toward the man in the three-piece suit.

His hands bounced away from Father Override, coming back feeling like he'd dipped his hands in hot grease.

Father Override looked defiantly up at Art. "Mr. Banks. Please. You're wasting your time, and your new talents."

Art swung one more time, but Father Override was right. His fists just couldn't reach him.

He waited until Art lowered his hands. "I am so glad you're here. We have unfinished business. But first we need to make sure you're safe."

Art felt his eyebrows raise questioningly as Father Override looked past him. "Stillborn! Give me some of your Born Again!"

Somewhere behind him, Art heard the woman grunt something. He heard more of Pentacle's magic, too, as well as a creaking sound as a wheelchair ran into the back of his right leg, causing his knee to buckle.

The right one being his bad leg, he instinctively grabbed for his thigh. It didn't hurt like it would have if he had been hit by a wheelchair at this time yesterday, though. It was a reflex that failed to keep him from falling to the ground without something to cushion him.

This something was the grandmother in the wheelchair.

He fell back on her, crushing the wheelchair and not wanting to think about what he did to the woman sitting in it. The wheels spread against the ground, their spokes splintering, the metal bending and tearing. Art felt something puncture the back of his right thigh.

He heard Father Override shout something, and more Born Again ran toward him. They ignored Art, which gave him a chance to reach down to see what had injured him. The woman's body was still and contorted in the chair. He tried not to think about it, no, not it. He tried not to think about her as he yanked a chunk of metal from his leg.

Thick blood fanned from Art's thigh, but it wasn't red. It was blindingly orange and thick, and landed with a batter-like splatter wherever it hit. And when it hit something, it caught fire.

Art tried to cover the wound, but the Born Again were surrounding him, and then pushing him back. He lost sight of the wheelchair as he tried to scramble to his feet while covering his leg with his hands. He could still hear Pentacle's magic, and he thought he saw Revenant running out of the bank.

And Voodoo Cowboy now stood on the light rail tracks in front of a stopped Max train. He wasn't firing at it anymore. Instead, he just watched it as it glowed orange and sprouted several spider-like legs from its front car to raise itself from its platform. Its connected cars broke free only a few feet off the ground and landed right-side up just off their tracks.

Voodoo Cowboy's guns were suddenly obscured. They were covered in dark shadow, and Voodoo Cowboy started shooting at the Max's new legs.

Something made a crunching clanging noise in front of Art. He brought his attention back to Father Override and the statue. One of the Born Again had run headfirst into Paul Bunyan's legs. Then she backed up, and Art expected to watch her throw herself against the statue again. Instead, she went to the ground on her hands and knees.

Another Born Again stepped on her back, and crouched. This one – a man in a too-tight business suit – held out his hand to the next Born Again.

As they continued to lift each other up the statue, Art managed to get to his feet. He took off his t-shirt and tied it around his leg to stop the magma-like blood spurting and starting little fires wherever it landed.

Revenant caught up to him. "Everyone in the bank has been turned into . . . what did you say they called them?"

"Born Again."

Revenant nodded. "They're all Born Again. What's happening out here . . . " His voice trailed off when he realized Voodoo Cowboy was fighting a walking Max train. His eyes widened before he looked back at Art. "Nevermind. Are you okay?"

Art instinctively reached for his leg again. The bleeding had stopped, but it still hurt, but not like his old football injuries. It just felt burnt.

He nodded and gestured to the statue. They both exchanged looks when they saw one of the Born Again – a twenty-something in a red polo and khaki pants – ascending the human stepladder to the top of Paul Bunyan.

Father Override shouted from the bottom. "Do it!"

Red Polo pulled his arm back and slammed it into Paul Bunyan's painted red-and-white shirt. Art heard a crunch over the noise and the foul singing in his head. He recognized the crunching as breaking bone, and he recognized the music as the same thing he heard at Blackstone Hall yesterday.

And he kept hearing those sounds as Red Polo continued to pound away at Paul Bunyan's shoulder, now using both hands.

Revenant said something about staying put before moving toward the statue. Father Override saw him coming, but turned his gaze back to Art.

CHAPTER 14

Art did not stay put. He charged Father Override again. He was a bit slower this time, not wanting to reopen the puncture wound in the back of his leg, but he felt his strength building with every step.

Revenant reached Father Override and Paul Bunyan before he did. The Solemn Judgment member didn't slow down, and somehow passed completely through the Born Again before him. And then he passed into the statue itself.

Father Override tore his eyes from Art and yelled out. "Stillborn! Stop playing with that woman! We need the heart!"

Stillborn was running out of Born Again. Voodoo Cowboy had incapacitated a handful, and most of the remaining were now serving as a living ladder. But there were still enough for her to command to surround the statue.

Pentacle's eyes glowed an angry sheen green as bubbles of energy flung themselves from her hands and that chest gem at Stillborn. Every time one of those attacks came close to Stillborn, a Born Again threw itself in its path instead.

Voodoo Cowboy continued firing at the Max train.

Revenant was somewhere inside that statue as far as Art could tell.

Stillborn found something on the ground, and bent to pick it up. She started laughing as she brought her scalpel up front of her and charged at Pentacle.

Pentacle leapt. Art watched her boots sparkle and suddenly Pentacle was floating several feet in the air.

Stillborn tried to stop herself but ran beneath her.

And when she was directly underneath her, Pentacle's feet dropped. She landed on Stillborn's shoulders, forcing the woman to the ground. Her just-recovered scalpel went sliding again.

It landed near Art's foot.

He picked it up, thinking it looked like a toy from his little sister's doctor's kit from when they were kids. It was so tiny.

No, his hands were so big. All of him was so much bigger now. So different.

The singing in his head struck a chord that vibrated against those

85

thoughts. A wave of anger flashed across his brain.

He found himself holding that scalpel and advancing on the two women.

Pentacle was back on the ground, her heavy breathing showing the toll this was taking on her. Her red hair stuck in clumps to the sides of her face and forehead. Stillborn, on the other hand, just rolled over to face the statue. Blood trickled from her mouth and nose, which sprayed out in a gasp when Art yanked her to her feet.

Stillborn refused to look at him. She kept turning her head to keep Paul Bunyan in her sight.

Pentacle reached for Stillborn, but Art yanked her up by her jacket collar. He wanted to shake this woman, make her undo what was done to him, make her hurt like he did.

No. Not like he did now. Like he used to. His right leg, his hip, and his back. They didn't hurt anymore. Not the same way. The sound in his head grated against the inside of his skull, and a dull burning ache filled his body, but it wasn't like it was with the football injuries. It was somehow better.

Or, at least, less painful.

But it was similar to the aches and pains he'd dealt with before. How many times did he come home from a football game banged up and bruised? This felt like that, but more intense. Nothing he couldn't handle.

"Put her down." Abigail glared at Art. "Put her down now, Art."

Stillborn didn't look back at her, or even at him. She kept her focus on Paul Bunyan. However, she did speak to him. "Yes. Put me down, Arturo."

A harsh clang caught the attention of Art and Pentacle. Stillborn was already looking in the direction of its source. Still holding her, Art looked at Paul Bunyan. Where Red Polo had been slamming his hands, wrists, and now-stubbed forearms into the statue were clumps of skin and bloody bones. Another clang, louder than the last, rang out as Red Polo slammed his forehead into the structure.

And then the blood flashed to fire, opening a hole in the shoulder of the 30-foot-tall statue.

Red Polo dove into the opening, and tumbled inside.

Stillborn finally turned to look at Art. "Put me down, Arturo."

Art finally did that very thing, but with a lot more force than anyone anticipated. He meant to yell, but a gnarled scream erupted from his throat and ripped past his lips instead. He lifted her as high as he could with one hand, and then spiked her like a football.

Pentacle screamed something at him, and while he couldn't make out what she said, he heard the noise clearly because as soon as Stillborn hit the ground, the sickly singing in his skull stopped.

The remaining Born Again started collapsing as if they were marionettes and suddenly their strings were cut.

Father Override's voice bellowed over the sound of Voodoo Cowboy's continuing gunshots. "Still Life! The statue!"

Pentacle broke off her scowl at Art and turned toward Paul Bunyan. Art did the same. Past the statue, he saw the spider legged-Max train lunge downward at Voodoo Cowboy who'd been standing his ground on the train tracks.

The six-shooter-slinging hero dodged out of the way when the nose of the Max slammed into the ground before him.

Art spotted Sill Life across the street, standing in the parking lot of the heavily-grafittied warehouse-like building on the other side of the intersection. Art could see his hands glowing that sick orange color as he faced their direction.

Pentacle moved for the statue before tossing a direction at him over her shoulder. "Stay put, Art."

Art felt his hands clench into fists again, but nodded.

And then the statue moved. Crumbling concrete and rending steel squealed as the cartoony sculpture of the legendary lumberjack jerked one of its legs free. Chunks of blue and white paint fell free as it took a step, first forward, then backward. Its second leg moved at its imaginary knee. Huge pieces of stone material fell away from the statue's waist as it twisted and bent over to pull at the axe standing in front of it.

Shrack! A glass-like bolt of light ripped from Pentacle's chest into the animated statue's waist.

"Mr. Williams is in there!" Art corrected himself. "Revenant! I mean Revenant! He's in there!"

Something thumped inside Paul Bunyan's form as the statue finally stood upright holding its axe above its head. Its caricature smile gleefully smiled as it swung the axe down like a golf club.

It missed Pentacle and Art, but scooped a handful of fallen Born Again off the ground and into the sky.

Pentacle turned her attention toward them, firing those verdant green bubbles off in their direction. She caught some of them.

Voodoo Cowboy started firing at the statue. Bursts of black smoke exploded on its surface. Paint and stonework shattered, but Art couldn't tell if Paul Banyan was taking any real damage.

The statue swung his axe again, this time leading with its axe blade. It didn't look sharp to Art, but that didn't stop it from crashing into the roof of the bank.

Somewhere in the distance, Art could hear sirens.

Was that the police or fire department? Ambulances maybe? What would any of them do that Solemn Judgment couldn't do? What could Solemn Judgment do? Art watched as Pentacle desperately tried to contain the damage to any people Paul Bunyan attacked with his concrete axe. Voodoo Cowboy continued firing at the statue, but it wasn't stopping it. He didn't know what happened to Revenant.

Still Life continued to watch from across the street. Art watched him. Still Life wasn't looking at Paul Bunyan.

He was watching Father Override.

Father Override stood at the spot that was just recently the base of the Paul Bunyan statue. The man had his back to Art, facing away to Sill Life. And he was talking. Not yelling at Still Life anymore. Just talking.

Like he was on the phone.

Art squinted at Still Life and saw he was doing the same thing.

He knew Pentacle told him to stay put, but he had to help. Somehow. If Solemn Judgment was going to help him, he wanted to help them, too.

He ran at Father Override, lowering his shoulder and bracing his head and neck for impact.

Paul Bunyan smashed the formerly-legged Max train into two pieces with its axe. It spun around again. Paul still smiled, but its painted-on teeth showed black damage from Voodoo's Cowboy's guns. It looked like the lumberjack had had several of his teeth knocked out.

Father Override turned to face Art. For the shortest of moments, Art saw an ear piece dangling from his target's ear. Father Override's eyes widened. Art's meaty shoulder slammed into the man's chest.

Paul Bunyan reached above its head with a free hand. More metal screamed as the statue continued to bend in ways it was never meant to.

Father Override slid on his back, his ear piece flying, his suit jacket tearing beneath him before he came to a stop.

Shrack! Shrack! Misshapen orbs of green floundered around him and Father Override.

Paul Bunyan brought his hand down and slammed it into his own stomach. Pieces of statue burst loose, showering down on Art, Father Override, and the collapsed Still Born. Pentacle threw up a shield to protect her from the concrete debris.

Art stomped over to Father Override and grabbed him by his shoulders. He easily lifted the man to his feet.

Father Override's words spit from a bloody lip. "You truly are strong, Mr. Banks."

Art shook him.

Paul Bunyan slammed its hand into its stomach again. More crunching sounds. More metal on metal, more concrete on concrete. More wreckage from the statue fell around them. A large chunk of red-and-white checker-pattern stonework clipped Art's head as it fell. It knocked against one of his horns and snagged an ear.

Art dropped Father Override and grabbed the side of his head. Scalding white hot blood slipped through his hand and fell to the ground in bursts of lava and smoke.

Father Override shakily got to his feet.

Paul Bunyan reached into its own stomach. Something squished inside the statue.

Blood from Art's ear splashed in a haphazard circle as he spun away from everyone. Pools of fire formed wherever the blood landed.

Everything went green for Art when one of Pentacle's bubbles formed around him.

Paul Bunyan pulled its hand out of its stomach. In its rubble fingers was a . . . clock?

It looked like a toy, like something out of *The Wizard of Oz* in the shape of a heart.

Father Override turned toward Still Life and made a slashing motion across his neck.

With one hand, Paul Bunyan swung its axe with all its might over the bank and into the residential neighborhood behind it. Pentacle lifted off the ground and moved after it.

Father Override took the heart-shaped clock from Paul Bunyan when it was handed to him.

Art tried to reach for him, but found Pentacle's magic kept him from leaving the confines of the shield. His hands pounded against the interior of the energy bubble.

Father Override smirked. "Until we meet again, Mr. Banks." He turned away. "Stillborn. To me."

Art stopped trying to free himself and watched helplessly as the woman he had just thrown into the ground slowly limp toward them. Father Override waited until she was close enough to extend a hand. She collapsed into his arm, blood streaming from somewhere along her scalp. Her dark hair stuck to her in chunks, hanging across her face.

Father Override extended a foot, and pressed a toe into one of the puddles of fire that formed out of Art's spilled blood. It sizzled against his designer shoe as he spread the fire into a small arc.

Still Life ran across the street, but was stopped when Voodoo Cowboy turned and shot him square in the chest. An explosion of dark energy brought Still Life down.

Stillborn and Father Override weren't watching, though. Instead, there were focused on the flames now leaping out of the small oval of fire in front of them.

Art reached for them again, but was helpless against Pentacle's magic. He could only watch as that fire turned into some sort of opening in the scorched cement.

Revenant finally emerged from the base of Paul Bunyan. The statue had stopped moving when Still Life stopped moving. Revenant looked around, and saw Art desperately reaching for Father Override and Stillborn.

But he was too far away to step them from stepping into the portal and disappearing in the fire.

CHAPTER 15

Father Override had the heart. It was ridiculous, but if Chambreau wanted this wind-up clock in the shape of a heart, then that is what he would deliver to him. Why he wanted this, or the rest of the items he was tasked to retrieve, he didn't understand.

When Chambreau called upon him last week to ask for "the viscera of a god, the heart of a giant, and the skull of a child," he thought he was joking. He went as far as questioning his benefactor, but Chambreau provided no answer. He demanded loyalty, and he demanded these three things.

So that is what James set about to find, after he formed a new group of Hounds. He found Luann and Jon serving time for some minor augmented human offenses, and with the abilities Chambreau granted him so many years ago, James made the Heckler siblings more powerful than they were before, and then aided them in their escape from Airway Heights. That part wasn't difficult.

Convincing them to follow his directions sometimes was.

And now Luann was making him doubt whether he should have bothered with the Heckler siblings at all.

"We have to go back!" She screamed at him, blood and saliva dribbling down her chin and puddling on the floor of the South Dome.

James took a step back to keep her from spitting on him. "When this is over, we will retrieve your brother."

She advanced on him, limping and holding one of her arms to her side. She glared at him with bloodshot eyes. "You left him behind!"

James raised a hand, halting her. "There is only one thing that matters here, Luann. One. And that isn't you, that isn't your brother, and that isn't even me."

She stopped. "But he's my brother."

"I freed him from his captors once before, and I'll do it again. After. We don't need him now."

"I need him."

"Not for what we have to do next."

James wasn't sure if he even needed Luann at this point. It was Chambreau that convinced him to find help in the first place. Was

Luann proving to be more trouble than she was worth?

"But then we'll get Jon back, right?" She sniffed and brushed her sweaty hair from her forehead.

James offered a meager nod. Maybe they would. He wouldn't need Jon after he retrieved the skull for Chambreau. He wouldn't need Luann, either, for that matter.

He felt a headache forming behind his eyes. James levelled a look at the woman. "Go get the chest."

She limped out of the South Dome.

James ascended the metal stairs to the telescope. Now that he'd retrieved the clock, or "heart of a giant," would Chambreau finally tell him why he needed these items? He assumed it was some sort of dark magic, but . . .

He pressed his face toward the eyepiece. Everything flashed hot, and then Chambreau was in the room with him again. James didn't understand how any of this worked, but Chambreau was older and especially wiser when it came to whatever dark arts that kept the two men alive for so long.

Alive. Is that what Chambreau was at this point? James knew he himself was alive. He breathed, he slept, he ate. But what of his old friend Edouard Chambreau?

"James, mon ami!" Chambreau extended his arms to him as James walked down the stairs.

Instead of accepting the embrace, though, James lifted the clock.

Chambreau's face split into a wicked smile. "Fantastique!" He reached for it.

A woman screamed.

Luann stood in the doorway connecting the South Dome to the Observation Room. She looked like she was about to drop the chest they'd retrieved from Blackstone Hall.

A darkness bled over Chambreau's face as he turned toward her.

James felt the strength in his legs leave him. He stumbled back, but caught himself on the stepladder's handrail.

Luann continued to scream as Chambreau advanced on her. "Father! What is it? Make it stop!"

The air was hot, and his vision swam before him. James shook his head, trying to clear his thoughts.

"Father! Help me!"

James dropped the clock. It crashed on the floor, the sound of metal on tile clanging through the South Dome. A snapping springing shot through his ears. He pulled back and tried to squeeze his eyes shut.

He found he couldn't. He couldn't look away. His eyes were locked on Chambreau as the man turned back toward him.

But he wasn't a man. And he wasn't Chambreau. It was barely man- or Chambreau-shaped. A collection of what looked like soaked-in-oil feathers and chunks of ivory held together but pulsing meat-pink ooze slowly slid on the floor toward James.

James wanted to twist, to turn, or just back up the stepladder. His hands, his feet, his knees would not bend. He tried to close his eyes against the thing in front of him, but even his eyelids refused to respond.

This thing was close to him now. It smelled like rubber and goat. Heat radiated off its form.

James felt his goatee sizzling. Tears blurred his eyes, making it even harder to make sense of what he was seeing. He felt sweat filling his ears and running down his neck. With every breath, his chest filled with a rancid air. James tried to cough, but even his lungs refused to cooperate.

The thing bent at what would have been its waist, and with a tendril formed of bone and sludge, it scooped the broken clock from the floor.

And then it slid away from him.

James felt his eyes move again, and his body followed. He rushed away from the thing with the clock and made for Luann.

Luann dropped the box. The ancient wood shattered, sending its contents spilling across the floor. Four jars made of stone rolled in separate directions, trailing dust and ages-old grit.

The thing that was not Chambreau lunged for the canopic jars, scooping them up with its horrid tentacles and absorbing them into its semi-man form.

James reached Luann and grabbed her shoulders. "Go. To the office."

Luann stared past James and at the thing slithering around the observatory. James looked over his shoulder and watched as it took another one of the canopic jars with a tentacle. Then the tentacle split another tendril lose that started working at opening the jar itself. Greasy strands wrapped around the jar's jackal-like top and started working it free.

James looked back at Luann and gave her shoulders a shake. "To the office."

Luann finally nodded.

Once she left, James made a point of closing the double-doors behind her. The creature in the room made a slurping sound, and then something snapped like breaking metal. James steeled himself to face whatever it was.

Edouard Chambreau, or something that looked vaguely like him, now stood in the center of the room, a self-satisfied smile sitting plainly on its lips.

James slowly made his way around the outer edge of the room. Keeping his back to the wall, he watched Chambreau. He . . . the thing watched him back, but eventually it did speak.

Or it made a noise. They weren't words. A screech like some dying animal erupted from the Chambreau-thing's mouth.

James felt its vibration in his head settle behind his eyes. The bridge of his nose felt like it was being pushed from within. He let himself lean against the wall, and gasped when the sound stopped and turned into actual speech.

"I've hated speaking French."

"What?"

"I've hated speaking it. My French is terrible."

James watched this thing's features. They looked like Edouard Chambreau's. Didn't they? The same beard, the same tiny eyes, the same . . . the same way he looked when he reentered James' life, but did he look the same way he did in San Francisco? Or the first time they reunited in Portland?

It spoke, its voice wavering between that of Chambreau's and something more high-pitched. "You owe me a service, James."

James slowly nodded.

"I want the skull. The clock and other nonsense mean nothing. But you must retrieve the skull for me."

The voice was different, of that James was sure. The French accent was completely gone. There was nothing but noise put through a vocal filter that sounded human enough, part Chambreau and part something else.

"I want the skull."

James blinked.

"I want the girl child's skull."

And then the thing was gone.

Luann ran to him. James did not stop her from grabbing on to his arms and trying to hold him. He heard her sobbing and staggered breath, and absurdly wanted to comfort the woman.

Or comfort himself.

What did he just witness? That was not his old friend and benefactor. The thing that appeared before him in the South Dome was something different. Something foreign and alien.

He glanced at the telescope before pulling himself away from Luann. She did not resist and let him go. She sniffed hard before letting herself sit down on the floot, crossing her legs and starting to rock herself.

James ignored her and ascended the steps to the telescope. He started to lean toward the eyepiece, but hesitated. Every time he looked into that telescope, it triggered his communication with Chambreau/not-Chambreau. Did he want to speak with it again? Did he need to?

Did he need to do anything it asked at this point? If it wasn't really his old friend after all, did he owe it anything?

Launn whimpered.

He spared her a glance before looking into the telescope.

James reached for the handrails as the sensation of falling overtook him, but he couldn't find them. His hands flailed at his sides. His vision went black, and his heart raced as he continued to fall downward, then inward, then he jolted to a complete stop.

"You." The voice still sounded so much like his old friend, but so different as well, as if multiple voices were layered upon one another as the speaker constructed its words.

James looked around desperately but could see nothing. It wasn't darkness. It wasn't blackness. There simply was nothing. He brought his hands in front of his face, he thought, but he could not see them. Looking down his body also showed him nothing.

"Why have you not left for the child?" The sentence was phrased as a question but spoken as a demand.

James swallowed back the panic he felt building in his gut before answering. "I want . . . I want answers."

"You are questioning me? Chambreau questioned me one too many times, and now he is dead."

Eduard was dead. Somehow, that did not surprise James at this point.

"Do you want to be dead as well?"

James felt his eyes blinking, but his vision didn't change. "No."

"Then what do you want to be?"

What did he want to be? When this first started all those years ago, Chambreau promised him power. Control. Wealth. Did he still want these things after all these years?

Yes. Yes, he did, he supposed. And he told the not-Chambreau thing as much.

That seemed to amuse it. "It doesn't matter what you want anymore. You owe me."

He started to nod, but the thing screamed again in his head. His scalp felt like it was about to crack.

"Not for the power. Not for anything you have, but for what you took from me!"

James started to ask why, but stopped himself.

The entity anticipated the question and offered a response nonetheless. "You say the skull belongs to an unnamed child in an unmarked grave. It's so much more than that, you fool, and I need you to find it."

"Why?" James couldn't stop the question from leaving his lips, so he tried to amend himself. "Why me?"

"Why you? You sound dangerously close to questioning me."

James shook his head. "No, I mean why did you chose me?"

Did that thing just laugh? "You're not listening. You owe me. You owe my family."

"I didn't think Edouard had any family."

"Not his. My husband's."

Husband? James didn't understand, and cautiously expressed as much.

"Danford Balch."

James recognized the name. It wasn't one he'd heard or even thought about in a long time, but it was one that was connected to his own history. When history remembered the name James Lappeus, Danford Balch's name wasn't too far behind.

"How is Danford Balch involved in this?"

"You're questioning me again, James."

The nothingness around him suddenly burst into blinding light. He tried to shield his face but the light shot through his hands and fingers, slamming into his eyes. It was blinding, and shot a wave of ice cold into his brain. Tendrils of freezing dread raced from his mind, down his neck and spine, and into his limbs. That sensation of falling overtook him.

He let himself scream, and only stopped when he landed on his back on the floor of the observatory.

His sight returned to him slowly. Luann was still on the floor of the South Dome. She crawled to him, and when she reached him, they both helped each other stand.

"Father? What happened?"

James looked at her. She was no longer crying, but tracks of tears streaked her face. Her nose had finally stopped bleeding, but he could see the bruising surfacing along her forehead and cheek. He brushed hair away from her eyes. "What did you see?"

Luann tried to step away, but he grabbed her arms and asked again. "What did you see?"

She shook her head. "You were just there, looking in the telescope and talking to yourself."

He released her. "I was here in the room the entire time?"

She nodded.

"You heard no other voice but mine?"

"Just you." She paused. "Who's Danforth Balch?"

"Danford. And it doesn't matter. We have work to do."

Luann straightened. "We'll get my brother?"

He started for the double doors leading out of the observatory.

She followed. "We will get my brother?"

As he pushed the doors open, he turned to look back at her. She could still be useful to him, especially if Solemn Judgment was going to keep interfering with them.

"When this is over, retrieving your brother will be my priority."

She nodded, accepting what James wanted her to hear. Whether he planned to free Jon Heckler from custody or not was not something he was considering at this point. His thoughts were occupied with Danford Balch and the Balch property. He knew where it was. It, too, was in Portland, which meant they would need to travel there through another of his portals.

Unfortunately, his portals weren't subtle, and he didn't want any more attention from Solemn Judgment or any other so-called superheroes.

Luann would be useful indeed. "Get yourself cleaned up, and meet me in the office in five minutes."

"Father?"

"You're going to the zoo."

CHAPTER 16

Deacon Andrews sat at the dining room table, one hand resting on a coffee mug, the other covering his tablet. The tablet hadn't stopped buzzing since he'd returned back here with Pentacle and Revenant. Art had already asked twice if Mr. Andrews was going to answer that incoming call.

After the Paul Bunyan statue toppled over into the intersection, Pentacle created a portal that brought the three of them back to Salem, leaving Voodoo Cowboy behind. Mr. Andrews was waiting for them, and immediately instructed them to sit. Art did as he was told, as did the other members of Solemn Judgment.

Pentacle was clearly angry, and if he was being honest with himself, he wasn't exactly happy with her, either. Abigail kept him from shaking answers from that Father Override character. She got in his way and actively stopped him. Solemn Judgment told him they would help him. But they didn't.

"This is perhaps my fault." Mr. Andrews touched a button on the tablet again, silencing the buzzing for a few moments. "I shouldn't have let you go."

Art exchanged a look with Mr. Williams, and then tried to make eye contact with Abigail. She avoided his eyes.

"But I encouraged it, and that is my responsibility."

The tablet started buzzing again.

Abigail slammed the table top with an open palm. "Will you please answer that, Grandfather?"

Mr. Andrews slid the tablet to Mr. Williams. "Take it in the other room please."

They all watched Mr. Williams silently take the tablet and leave.

Art took a deep breath and let it out slowly. "I am sorry."

Mr. Andrews began to speak, but his granddaughter interrupted him.

"No. I'm sorry. I should not have encouraged any of this. My grandfather should have known better, but I'm the field leader. You had no business out there with us." She leveled her gaze at her grandfather. "You had no business letting him out of his room."

Art slid back in his chair. "Wait a minute. You brought me here. You could have just left me in Portland."

Mr. Andrews shook his head. "That's not how we do things."

"How you do things? You said you'd help me."

"We did." Mr. Andrews stood and started circling the table. "And we will, if we can. You need to understand, though, that we have other pressing responsibilities."

"Other responsibilities?" Art started to stand.

Abigail snapped to her feet. "Stay seated." Her eyes flashed a dark green.

Art remained seated.

Abigail's grandfather continued. "We will try to help you. I will make it a priority, after these other responsibilities have been dealt with."

Art shook his head. "What happened to the other guy?"

"The other guy?" Mr. Andrews looked to Abigail.

She sighed. "Voodoo Cowboy took him into custody."

Her grandfather stopped his slow circular pacing around the table. "I didn't realize . . . "

"You know that's his neighborhood, Grandfather."

"No. I mean I didn't realize there was a survivor."

Art had started to grew accustomed to his larger size, but in that moment, he felt smaller than he'd ever had before. "Survivor? Only . . . one?"

Abigail finally looked him in his eyes. "So far. Voodoo Cowboy said he'd contact us with any updates." She flicked her eyes to her grandfather and back again. "But it doesn't look good."

Art sunk even further into his chair.

Abigail continued. "I know you wanted to help, or at least help yourself. We understand, and even expected that after we learned a bit more about you."

"About me?"

She nodded. "Last night, Hence learned more about who you are, Arturo."

"Just Art."

"Fine. Last night, Art, Hence made some inquiries online and we know you're a good person. No matter what happened in Kenton, we know that." She reached for him with a cautiously reassuring hand. "And you know that, too, right?"

He numbly nodded.

"Father Override and Stillborn got away, but we haven't given up. And we haven't given up on you, Art."

Mr. Andrews returned to his chair. "When Hence Williams came to us, we agreed to help him, too. At the time, Solemn Judgment was just Abigail and her brother. When her brother left, Hence agreed to start helping in the field."

Art looked to Abigail. "You have a brother?"

She nodded, but her grandfather continued.

"And when we can, we still look for answers for Hence. We'll do the same for you. In the meantime, you have to decide . . . " His voice trailed off, and his eyes drifted into the distance.

"Grandfather?"

Art watched as the muscles in the older man's necks bunched into thick cords. His shoulders tightened, and his eyes went wide.

"Grandfather!" Abigail leapt from her seat, but by the time she reached his side, his muscles and eyes relaxed.

He looked at her and offered a meager smile. "I'm fine, but I just felt something powerful."

"I could tell. Are you sure you're okay?"

He patted her hand. "I'll be fine, but I need a map. Now."

Art watched Abigail practically run from the room.

Mr. Andrews answered Art's question before he could ask it. "I will be fine, Art. It is my gift."

"Gift?"

"You didn't think my granddaughter and Hence are the only two members of Solemn Judgment supernaturally gifted, did you?"

"I hadn't really thought about it."

"We try hard to keep most people from thinking about it. Abigail and Hence know, of course. Abigail's brother, my late wife and daughter. And the folks in Washington, of course."

"Washington?"

"We're registered as part of the Nixon Protocols, Mr. Banks." He offered a sly smile. "We don't tell them everything, though. For example, we haven't told them about you, yet."

The thought of Art's name being on some government list somewhere hadn't occurred to him yet, and it wasn't something he wanted to think about.

"What can you do?" Art cringed at how childish the question

sounded.

"About Washington?"

"No. I mean, you said you had a gift?"

"Do you know what dousing is?"

Art wasn't sure, but let Mr. Andrews continue.

"Or, better yet, when you throw a stone in a pool of water, the waves ripple out from the point of impact. As the waves move away from that point of impact, the ripples get smaller and smaller." He illustrated with his hands moving away from an imaginary point in front of him. "I can feel those waves."

"So someone threw a rock in a lake somewhere?"

Mr. Andrews smiled and reminded Art of one of his old high school teachers. "Imagine the rock is some sort of supernatural event. When something happens that by all rights has no right to happen according to our natural world, it makes a series of invisible waves. And when those resulting ripples hit me, based on their direction and intensity, I can usually tell where that supernatural splash took place. Especially if I have a map."

As if waiting for her cue, Abigail returned. She spread a map on the tabletop, making sure to place it close enough to her grandfather to see.

The older man stood and placed his palms on the map. He closed his eyes. His arms went loose as his hands slid over its surface, gliding together from spot to spot. Eventually, his hands slowed and he lifted them so that just his forefingers were barely touching the map. "Here." He opened his eyes.

Abigail leaned forward. "The zoo?"

Mr. Andrews nodded. "There."

Abigail looked to Art and appeared to give him a once over before turning back to her grandfather.

"What about him?"

Art straightened, trying to feel tall again.

CHAPTER 17

Hence sat at his desk, holding the tablet, talking with Voodoo Cowboy. "And they've taken him into custody?"

Troy Norris nodded back at him through the screen. "I made sure he was out, and the police took him away."

"That was fast."

"When I told them what he could do, they didn't waste any time. How's the new guy?"

Hence shook his head. "Art? Other than insisting on calling me Mr. Williams all the time, he's about as adjusted as someone in his position can be, I suppose."

"That's not what I meant . . . Mr. Williams."

"Don't you start."

Troy flashed a grin at him, but let it fade quickly. "You know what I mean, though. Did you tell him about the woman in the wheelchair?"

Hence felt his own face darken. "Not yet. It wasn't his fault."

"I know. None of those people survived. We tried."

"And I'll tell Art that. He's a good kid, though, and I suspect he'll blame himself for the old woman at least."

"Keep calling him 'kid' and he'll keep calling you 'Mr. Williams.'"

Hence tried to smile, appreciating Troy's attempt to keep the dread seriousness of the matter at bay.

"Why don't you come out to Salem, Troy? It might help Art."

"You know that's not a good idea. Deacon and I don't get along."

"I know. But if it helps the kid . . . "

"There's a lot of collateral damage in the neighborhood I need to help with right now, Hence. Maybe later, when this is all cleaned up."

"Okay." Hence heard in Troy's voice that he had no intention of coming to Salem. He was right. He and Deacon did not see eye to eye, although Hence suspected the animosity came more from Deacon than it did from Troy.

"Hang on a second." Troy turned away from the screen. Hence could see he was sitting in a van, and the man's attention was focused on something to the side. Troy glanced back at him. "Are you hearing this?"

"I can only hear you."

"Hang on." The tablet's image of Troy shook as he repositioned it. From Troy's end of the conversation, Hence heard another voice. It sounded like it was coming from a speaker or a radio. "I can't make it out. Something about . . . the Oregon Zoo?"

Troy looked back at Hence as he turned down the radio. "There's something happening at the zoo. Sounds like the same people we just dealt with out here."

"I'll let Abby and Deacon know."

"And I'll probably see you there."

Hence left his room, taking the tablet with him.

CHAPTER 18

Abigail watched Art closely as they, along with Hence, arrived in the amphitheater lawn of the Oregon Zoo. Before they left Salem, Art promised all he wanted to do was help, and she believed him. Hence was the same way when he joined Solemn Judgment, and he had more than proved himself since then.

But what Hence could do was significantly less lethal than what Art was proving himself capable of.

Art looked lost and confused. They found a new t-shirt for him before they left, but it was at least two sizes too small for him. He seemed awkward, but eager. She noted that he'd already balled his hands into massive fists.

She exchanged a look with Hence. He nodded back to her before manifesting his sword.

A screaming red-tailed monkey ran in front of them, its simian paws grabbing the sides of its heads.

The three of them watched it run and hop into the elephant enclosure.

Art grabbed the sides of his own head.

An elephant roared.

Somewhere nearby, a hawk screamed angrily.

With a flick of her fingers, Pentacle erected a shield around the three of them just as a group of brown-bodied white-faced ducks charged in their direction.

"Abby?" Hence held his khopesh at the ready, but did not swing at the rabid ducks.

"Pentacle."

"Can we argue about names later? Is this what your grandfather felt?" Revenant gestured at the ducks that had stopped to stare mindlessly at them.

She looked around. Other animals were roaming the zoo grounds. Some were running, like the group of goats charging what looked like a grade school field trip, while others simply shambled back and forth across a walkway, like the three orangutans wobbling on their feet, clutching their ears.

"You said Voodoo Cowboy heard about this?" Pentacle raised a hand, ready to deflect the angry goats with one of her witch bolts if they got too close to those school kids.

"He said there was a disturbance, and that woman Stillborn was spotted."

Pentacle didn't like the look that just crossed Art's face.

"He also said he'd reach out for more back-up. After Kenton this morning, he didn't want any more fatalities. I didn't disagree."

She wished he hadn't used the word "fatalities" just then.

Art didn't seem to notice. He was just holding his head, watching, scanning the zoo.

He was looking for Stillborn.

Pentacle really wanted to trust Art, but wanting to and being able to were two different things. What happened at Kenton with the woman in the wheelchair wasn't his fault. She wouldn't have survived more than likely even if he didn't collapse onto her.

It was his actions toward Stillborn and Father Override that worried her.

She was of two minds. On the one hand, stopping them was what they intended to do. On the other hand, she saw the look in Art's eyes, and it wasn't human. Pentacle realized the ridiculousness of that thought. Of course Art wasn't human anymore. He'd been changed Father Override, and if she was being honest with herself, she didn't know if Solemn Judgment could help change him back.

Having seen what he did in Kenton, she did not want to leave him alone with her grandfather. She knew he could take care of himself, she knew, and their home was protected by all the powerful magics she knew. But bringing Art him to the Oregon Zoo? Was that the wisest choice?

The ducks jumped at the sound of gunshots.

That had to be Voodoo Cowboy.

When the foul fowls settled, they charged Pentacle's shield. Their beaks bounced off the green energy, dotting it with flecks of blood and tiny tufts of feathers from the ducks' heads.

The sound of Art's breathing grew into a growl. He raised his fists.

Revenant turned toward him and raised a hand. "Don't!"

Art punched at the magical defense.

She cursed herself for not thinking to strengthen the interior of the shield. It could deflect blows from outside, but from inside, in order for her own attacks to pass through it, she had to keep it weak. And when Art swung at it from within? It shattered. Shards of hardened light and cool green split and exploded outward. The ducks flew back from the force of her shield blasting apart, trailing feathers and blood.

Art screamed and ran south toward the aviary.

Revenant started after him, but hesitated and looked to Pentacle for direction.

She nodded.

Revenant ran after him.

The group of grade school students and their chaperones had gotten away from the goats, but now an angry flamingo, its typically pink feathers now streaked runny red from its head down its long neck, snapped at them.

Shrack! Pentacle fired a bolt in the flamingo's direction. It flapped its wings and half-ran, half-flew away from the children.

She waved the teachers and the students toward her as she concentrated and pushed several feet off the ground. Some of the children stopped, so she tried to smile at them. A handful of them smiled back. Then all of them, smiling or not, started yelling and pointing at her.

Pentacle rotated in the air. She wasn't traditionally a flyer, but she was able to levitate for short periods of time. Maneuvering wasn't a strength for her, but she could rotate like her grandfather's record player. The kids and now some of the adults were pointing past her.

She spun in time to see the bald eagle screaming at her, its talons pointed at her face.

Pentacle ducked, doing her best to keep her balance. The eagle caught a handful of her hair. It yanked, and she felt hair rip from her scalp.

The eagle flapped its wings frantically as it scooped through the air and came back around. Pentacle dropped her left hand and started weaving invisible threads between her fingertips. The bird's thick legs pointed its taloned feet at her.

She could just blast the bald eagle and be done with it, but not in front of the children, and more importantly, possessed or not – she could see the smudges of blood along the sides of its sleek skull – it was still a bald eagle.

It shook its mighty wings at her and charged.

Pentacle flung her hand at the bird. The magical threads, still connected to her fingertips, wrapped around its neck and one of its wings. She closed her hand, and yanked. The bald eagle chirped as it flew uncontrolled through the air.

When she had whipped the bald eagle behind her, she shook her hand and the magical threads glowed blindingly white-green. A sound like an electric rip vibrated from her fist down the connecting threads of energy and into the bald eagle. It screeched before it completely vanished.

She opened and closed her hand quickly, the magic melting away. Then she realized the field trip group was staring at her. Pentacle tried to smile again. "It's okay. I just sent it away."

Pentacle didn't know if she could teleport another being away like that, and she wasn't entirely sure where the bald eagle ended up, but at least she didn't actually kill the country's national bird in front of a bunch of third- and fourth-graders.

A large animal made an even larger sound somewhere behind her. She turned again, and this time the threat was not in the air. It was on the ground, charging in her direction.

A clearly irritated and also possessed rhinoceros thundered its way down the walkway.

She started to lower herself to make a barrier between her and the field trip group that should have run off by now. When her feet hit the ground, she heard the exploding sounds of Voodoo Cowboy's gunshots.

The rhino slowed as puffs of dark blue smoke burst on its back side. Voodoo Cowboy was speeding around the corner behind it on a golf cart, firing.

More hits on the rhino's thick skin slowed the animal to a march, and then a walk. Pentacle touched the gem at her chest and called upon the magic deep inside herself. A cooling wave of soft green light burst from her chest, showering the rhinoceros' head and shoulders with a cascade of controlling magic.

Voodoo Cowboy's golf coat screeched to a halt. He hopped out, a six-shooter still aimed at the beast. After three more shots, and Pentacle's continued magical assault, the rhinoceros finally settled and laid down on its side. Panting heavily, it closed its eyes.

CHAPTER 19

Revenant dodged a diving bat and let himself slip through a pack of angry naked mole rats as he chased after Art. A pair of zookeepers ran desperately in his direction. He tried to flag them down, but they ignored him and kept running. When he heard the roar, he realized why they were running.

A lion leapt across his path. Its disheveled main hung loose around its head. Like the other animals he'd already seen since they arrived at the zoo, it also had two wounds, one on either side of its head. Blood trickled down the lion's face. Its eyes started blankly at Revenant before it shook its heavy head and charged him.

Revenant's khopesh flashed in his hand. He stood defiantly in front of the lion, staring into the feline's eyes as its massive paws and thick muscled legs powered the animal toward him.

It wasn't really a two-handed weapon, but Revenant gripped the sword's handles with both hands anyway. He twisted slightly as his waist, and pulled the blade back.

The lion squealed and came to an abrupt halt.

Art stood behind it, grabbing it by its tail.

Revenant let out an anxious breath.

The lion turned to face Art. Seeing the two massive creatures face off made Revenant acutely aware of his own size. He tightened his grip on his sword and took a step forward.

Art pulled on the lion's tail. The animal's toes spread wide as it tried to find purchase on the asphalt. Its claws scraped on the ground. Blood trickled down its cheeks.

Revenant relaxed his grip on his sword while Art swung the lion away, but tightened it again when he realized Art's eyes were now locked on him.

"Easy, kid." Revenant prepared to let his body lose its form completely as Art took several steps toward him.

Art blinked. "What? No. I'm okay now."

"You sure?"

Art looked down at his hands and made a point of relaxing his fists. "I am. The sound doesn't bother me anymore."

"The sound?"

"Stillborn. Or that Override guy. I can hear their song in my head, but I got used to it."

"And you're . . . good?"

Art nodded.

An otter ran by, stopping only to spit and chirp at them before running off.

Art cracked his knuckles. "All of them are like that."

"The animals?"

Art nodded. "It seems like the same kind of thing Stillborn did before at Blackstone Hall and at the statue."

Revenant agreed with the kid. "Have you seen Stillborn?"

"Not yet, but I can tell she's here somewhere. I'll find her."

He chose his next words carefully. "And what are you going to do if you do find her, Art?"

Art's jaw muscles clenched. "Bring her down."

"You mean bring her in."

"That, too."

"We take her into custody, kid. That's what we do."

"I know. And we need her to fix me."

Revenant slowly nodded. "Right. Her and Father Override."

"I haven't seen him yet. Hey, look out." Art suddenly reached over Revenant's head, catching the grey gull diving at the back of his neck. He tossed the angry bird away. It caught itself with its wings and flew toward the gift shop.

Revenant could hear gunfire somewhere in the distance. That had to be Voodoo Cowboy. He hoped it wasn't the local police. Something like that otter or bird, the locals could handle, but the lion Art so easily dealt with?

And who could or would deal with Art if this sudden change didn't last?

"You said you heard Stillborn in your head?"

Art tapped one of his temples. "I still do."

"Do you think you can track her, follow her somehow?"

Art thought for a moment before slowly nodding. "I think I can."

"Then let's go. And watch out for those penguins."

CHAPTER 20

Art easily side-stepped the penguins waddling toward them from the pizza parlor. Of the seven of them, only the last penguin in the group stopped to look at him and Revenant. Art growled at it, and it skittered away with its companions.

He'd been to the zoo once before when he first moved to Portland for school. Back then, the animals weren't free roaming. Every animal, every beast, and even every large insect he'd passed since they got here this time were out of their enclosures, and all of them had those matching wounds at their temples. They'd all been turned into Stillborn's Born Again.

None of the people he'd encountered, though, had been. The people working at the coffee stand, the customers in the gift shop, even the zoo employees were all unaffected. But they were being harassed by the animals.

Art burst out of Pentacle's defensive shell when he felt Stillborn's call. He'd been checking the sides of his head repeatedly. Even though they felt like the familiar wounds had opened up, there was no blood. There were no cuts. And yet, that horrid sound was louder in his head now than it was earlier today in Kenton, or even yesterday at his dorm.

That was only yesterday. Art knew that it had been less than twenty-four hours since he watched the sides of his friend's head open before meeting Stillborn herself, but he'd grown very used to this new body of his. He was starting to strangely feel at home in it.

It was, after all, his body, just . . . changed.

The fact that he was accepting it as his body now bothered him less now than it did last night, but that bothered him more.

Stillborn and Father Override were responsible for what had happened, and they didn't lie to him. His football injuries from last year no longer hurt. He didn't feel the weakness in his leg, the hardware in his knee didn't click anymore. His hips and lower back didn't ache.

Did he owe them for this?

Stillborn's discordant tone rang inside his skull. Outside his skull, his elongated ears could hear better than he had before. He could hear the strangled coughs of the condors as they left the aviary and attacked a couple who had just ordered a pair of elephant ears at a snack bar. A half-dozen seals barked at the Zoo Train before slamming themselves against it and derailing it off its tracks. Two red pandas huff-quacked at a tarantula before climbing to the roof of the event space near the zoo entrance.

The chaotic noises helped to center Art. Hearing Stillborn's call when they first arrived sent panic surging through him, but hearing all the animals react to Stillborn overrode that head noise enough for Art to be able to regain control.

"Can you find Stillborn?" Revenant's head swiveled back and forth down either way of the pathway. "Is she in the zoo?"

Art braced himself as he pushed the agitated sounds of the zoo's residents out of his mind. That weird moaning-howling was still there, and his admittedly limited experience told him that that meant Stillborn was still here.

He nodded. "Somewhere nearby."

Something that sounded like a heavy galloping horse was getting closer to them. Revenant didn't seem to notice, but from his height, Art could see over him and some of the trees in the way.

A giraffe, blood streaming down its neck, heaved toward them. Its body led it around a trashcan and up an incline; its head followed on its long neck. It started bleating when it saw Art.

Revenant finally heard the giraffe and turned to face it. He lifted his sword. Art thought Revenant's body seemed somewhat transparent as the man stepped to intercept the giraffe.

The giraffe's bleating turned into a screaming grunt.

Revenant stood his ground, but when the giraffe was only a few feet from him, he dropped to his knees and slashed with his sword.

It passed into the giraffe's legs. The sword didn't actually cut the animal. The blade just disappeared in the giraffe's body as it ran over Revenant. No, not over Revenant. It ran through him, then slowed and stomped at the ground where the man with the sword stood.

Revenant slashed again, this time passing his sword into the giraffe's right legs, and then its belly. The giraffe stomped furiously, but it found nothing solid to connect with as Revenant continued his attack.

The sword attack was slowing the creature, but it wasn't stopping it. It spit and bleated as Revenant kept slashing at it.

Art finally reached for the giraffe, cutting it off in mid-grunt when he grabbed its neck. Gently, he squeezed, feeling the animal strain against him, but listening carefully to the sound of its slowing breaths.

"Art! What are you doing?"

He ignored Revenant and kept applying gentle pressure to the animal's neck. Finally, the giraffe's eyes rolled back in its head. Its head dipped and its neck went limp. Art immediately stopped squeezing, and helped to lay the giraffe onto the ground. He could still hear it breathing when he straightened to see Revenant watching him carefully.

"It's okay. I – "

"Choked it out?"

Art defensively nodded.

"That's better than nothing." He passed his sword from one hand to the other. "I wasn't having much of an effect on it anyway."

Art stopped hearing Revenant in that moment. Instead, he heard Stillborn's voice. Since Revenant didn't react to it, Art assumed it was inside his head. She called to him by name, another indicator to him that Revenant was not the intended audience.

Arturo. Come to me.

"Art? What is it?"

Art tried to remember the he should apologize to Mr. Williams later for putting up a finger to shush him.

You belong with us, Arturo. Join me at the entrance, and we'll go to Father Override together.

Go to Father Override?

Did that mean he wasn't here?

He looked around. Three gazelles were headbutting one another, each collision fanning droplets of blood onto each other. A large monitor lizard of some sort waddled its way toward a lighting fixture. A groundskeeper ran from a scampering crocodile. There were gunshots, some of those sounds Pentacle's magic made, and a new sound like a laser blast from a science fiction movie rang out from the amphitheater.

"Are we losing you, kid?"

Art blinked hard and looked down at Revenant. "Stillborn's here. But I don't think Father Override is."

"Can you track her?"

"She's calling me."

Revenant hefted his sword. "Then lead the way."

Art closed his eyes and tried to tune out the sounds of the animals, the screaming, the gunshots and other blasts. The sound of fist fights and tackles erupted somewhere behind him and to the left. Sirens were approaching ahead of them in the direction of the entrance.

The penguins made their way back around, and were now waddling behind Art and Revenant as they made their way toward the zoo's covered entrance. Whatever employees that had been working the ticket booths had already abandoned their post. An orangutan sat in the plexiglass enclosure, rocking and holding its head. It ignored them as the semi-transparent Revenant and the incredibly solid Art approached.

"There." Art pointed at the building just behind the ticket entrance area. The large building sat along the side of the asphalt walkway, its roof collecting hawks and condors. The birds all sat vigilantly, watching the two of them approach.

I see you. Art heard Stillborn's voice in his head. It clanged against the sound of his own pounding heart and rushing blood. *I see you, and you're not alone. Lose him.*

Art's pace slowed.

Revenant noticed. "What's wrong?"

"She sees you. She sees me."

"And?"

Art looked around and let his eyes settle on the birds settling on the building's roof. A duck frantically flapped its wings to join them. "I think she can see me through them."

"Is she in the building?"

"I think so."

"Then let's go."

Art put up a hand to block Revenant, forgetting for a moment that he could have just walked through his outstretched arm if he wanted to.

Revenant did stop, though.

"She wants me."

"And I know you want to get your hands on her." Revenant paused to watch a column of penguins march past them and start making their way to the parking lot. "I'm not letting you go alone, kid."

Art shook his head. "I'm good. Really. Should you . . . stop the cats or something?"

Revenant raised his eyebrows. "Stop the cats?"

Art pointed at a group of random cats darting back and forth in front of two zoo employees. One of the employees held her forearm. It was dripping blood. The cats seemed to be playfully shepherding the two employees further into the zoo.

And toward the lion Art had dealt with earlier. No longer looking dazed, it stood proudly at the end of this particular path, licking its lips as the smaller cats worked to deliver the humans to it. Whenever one of the zoo employees tried to skirt around a particular cat, a different one leapt at her, scratching up their leg, hissing and biting.

Revenant sighed. "Fine. But stay here."

Art barely waited long enough for Revenant to take just a few steps toward the big-cat-little-cats situation before turning and heading toward the bird-covered building.

CHAPTER 21

"I called everyone I could." Voodoo Cowboy yelled to be heard over the sound of the whining golf cart and his six-shooter.

Shrack! A zigzagging bolt of green light fired from Pentacle's pointed fingers toward a porcupine. It caught the animal, sheering a handful of quills from its body. The porcupine chattered its teeth at them as it regained its balance and continued moving toward the golf cart.

"Even Seattle?" Pentacle kept an eye on the porcupine, and prepared to fling another spell in its direction.

"I didn't know who could get here quickly." Voodoo Cowboy fired at the porcupine. It was pushed back several feet as a burst of purple dust hit it in its face. It sneezed at them.

"I thought I saw Blindspot earlier." She flung another bolt at the porcupine. Shrack! "Who else?"

Voodoo Cowboy shrugged. "Slaphappy. Deadfall. Showdown."

"You have Deadfall on speed dial?"

She noticed he didn't answer her question and fired at the porcupine again. The golf cart was starting to slow as its motor whined even louder.

"I don't even like Showdown. Too showy with his handguns."

She made no comment as he fired again.

"I don't know who else is here, but a lot of them are helping people in the parking lot and working crowd control."

Shrack! The porcupine finally gave up and rolled onto its side. "Have you seen Art?"

"The big red guy you brought to the statue? How could you lose track of someone that size?"

The golf cart came to a begrudging halt and she stepped out. "He's got some kind of connection with Stillborn and Father Override. Grandfather thought it would be a good idea to bring him, but he may have lost control."

Gunshots – not Voodoo Cowboy's, but actual gunpowder-firing gunshots – filled the air near the insect building.

"See?" Voodoo Cowboy checked his own weapons. "Showdown is just showing off. I told him to stay down at the Max stop."

"You called a sharpshooter here, and then told him to go to the underground train stop?"

"I knew he'd show up whether I called him or not, so I tried to put him where he'd do the least amount of damage."

Pentacle knew telling Grandfather that Voodoo Cowboy called as many of the nearby aug-humans, including someone non-registered like Deadfall, was going to be a hard conversation. She liked Troy, and really wanted to see him and Solemn Judgment work together more in the future, but this wasn't going to help.

She didn't have time to worry about that now. The porcupine screamed and hopped to its feet. The animal shook its head violently before facing her and charging.

Voodoo Cowboy fired. So did Pentacle. The porcupine was pushed back and collapsed in a handful of dust and quills. Pentacle kept a magical shield around the two of them, and tried to watch the path as the two of them cautiously approached the still animal.

"I hate to say it, Pentacle, but if the animals are like the folks in Kenton . . . "

She had been thinking the same thing. "None of them recovered?"

Voodoo Cowboy shook his head.

Pentacle didn't want to consider what that meant for Art.

CHAPTER 22

Art felt the eyes of the hawks and condors tracking him as he approached the building, but he knew it wasn't the birds watching.

It was Stillborn.

Join me, Arturo.

Art reached for the double doors, and prepared to duck to let himself in. He'd been ducking through doorways at Mr. Andrews' house, and had gotten used to making sure that not just his head cleared doorframes, but also his ears and horns. He hesitated to admit to himself he'd gotten used to that because he didn't want to stay this way any longer than he had to.

That was true, right? He didn't like this? He'd need things to go back to how they were before.

Which meant getting his hands on Stillborn.

She was waiting for him on the other side of the doors. An ugly bruise spread across the side of her face and her hair was crusted to the side of her head. She looked like she'd been crying, but as she made eye contact with Art, she smiled.

"Come to me!" Her hands flashed in front of her. Silver glinted in her hands. She charged him with her scalpels.

In a curtain of feathers and blood, the birds roosting on the roof jumped free and dove as one feathery form at him.

Art put his muscular arms in front of him to halt Stillborn's attack. He easily blocked her, avoiding being cut. When the birds reached him, however, had had to flail his hands around to keep them from drawing blood while still keeping Stillborn at bay. A red-tailed hawk slipped in and dug into his wrists with its talons. Hot blood spouted from where the bird cut him, spraying it and setting it on fire. It tried to fly away as the magma-like blood dripped from its legs and wings.

Stillborn slashed at Art, ignoring the burning bird. Art kept trying to keep the blades from his skin, but when a condor starting ripping at his scalp, he reached up to stop it. The cool metal of one of Stillborn's scalpels opened a cut several inches long in Art's forearm.

Blood fanned white hot from Art's arm. He clapped his free hand over the spouting magma. It burned his hand, but he squeezed tight, leaving him undefended when Stillborn slashed at him again. He tried to turn away, but her scalpel cut across his elbow.

Another hawk flew at his face.

Stillborn laughed.

Somewhere someone was firing a gun.

A polar bear rumbled nearby.

Art ducked the hawk, leaned back, and avoided another slash from Stillborn's scalpels.

"Stop it!" Art wanted to defend himself with his hands, but doing so would spray the birds and even Stillborn with his burning blood. But he had to at least try avoiding their attacks.

Stillborn lunged at him.

He turned and blocked her with his shoulder, knocking her to the ground. Her scalpels bounced away from either hand.

Art bobbed his head away from another one of the birds dipping toward him as he tried to keep any of his blood from hitting anyone or anything. His elbow burned as he unfolded his arm to press the cut against his chest. His t-shirt caught fire, but he didn't feel it.

Stillborn struggled to sit up. As she did, three dwarf mongooses scampered toward her. She scooped one of them up and threw it at Art's face.

Art caught the animal as gracefully as he could. He tried to set it back on the ground, but it bit the webbing between his thumb and forefinger. The mongoose screamed as a tiny jet of flaming blood burst from the broken skin.

Stillborn stood and clapped her hands together. The mongooses, the birds, all the animals near her suddenly stopped. The birds came to land on either side of her. The pair of red pandas rolled to her feet. Stillborn glowered at Art through disheveled hair.

"Arturo Banks. Former football star. Killer of animals and women."

Her voice rang in his head.

"Broken. Damaged goods. A failure."

Art let his burning t-shirt fall away.

The two remaining mongooses glared at him.

He could hear galloping hooves somewhere in the zoo. It didn't sound like another giraffe. This was someone on horseback.

Another gunshot, but this one further away and somehow somewhere below him.

Art felt his wounds seeping the thick flammable substance that was now apparently his blood.

Stillborn was both in his head and in front of him. "When will you give up?"

Art looked around. Everywhere his blood touched had burst into tiny fires. The mongoose that bit him earlier lay stretched out in a smoldering mess of burnt fur. A dead hawk lay several feet away. A smoking tarantula lay dying as its abdomen smoked.

"Come with me to Father Override. Let's fix this."

She lifted her arms to either side and opened her fingers.

"Let's fix you."

Art couldn't tell if the howling he heard now was in his head or an actual zoo animal in distress.

Stillborn stepped toward him. "Let's go to Father Override."

Art covered his ears. The song was in his head again. His temples felt hot as his blood rushed through ears. He squeezed his eyes shut, but that only made the sound louder and balefully worse.

When he snapped them open again, Stillborn stood before him. She looked up into his eyes. "Let's leave."

Her stared back at her bloodshot eyes. "Leave?"

"To go see Father Override."

"Father Override. He's . . . "

"He's not here, Arturo."

He tried to shake the discordant music from his head. "Where is he?"

"The Witch's Castle."

Art knew where that was. It was nearby, but it wasn't here.

Father Override wasn't here.

He lifted his head, and took a step back. What was all this then, if he wasn't here?

As soon as the answer came to him, all traces of Stillborn's horrid song evaporated.

This was a distraction.

"Are you ready to find real purpose, Arturo? To become a Hound like me and my brother?"

Blood trickled down his arm, scorching his abdomen and pants. The flow of blood had slowed, but he still ached. He lowered his head and let both of his hands fall to his sides.

He nodded at Stillborn.

Stillborn took him in an embrace.

He hugged her back.

And didn't stop.

Stillborn struggled against him, huffing as he tried to spin her around to wrap an arm around her neck. He felt something snapping at his legs. One of the hawks flew to the top of his head and wrapped its talons around one of his horns. He shook it free, and continued to maneuver Stillborn around so he could get a good grip on her throat from behind.

She gasped, and might have even said his name, but he didn't allow her enough air to speak too loudly. Something with dozens of tiny legs crawled up his back. He ignored it and finally slipped his upper arm against Stillborn's neck. It felt so small and delicate against his skin.

Stillborn stomped at his feet. He didn't feel it. She tried to dig her chin into his bicep. He ignored it. She reached for his face.

And he winced when her fingernails tore at his face beneath his right eye.

But he didn't let go.

Blood oozed down his cheek, and when it hit her hand, it burst into flame. Stillborn screamed and tried to twist away.

Art tightened his grip. He turned his head to the side to keep from bleeding directly on her, but he refused to let her go.

The woman's struggles slowed. Whatever was crawling on his back fell off. Some of the birds flapped their wings to try to get away, but eventually slumped and drifted to the ground. Some animal Art couldn't identify screamed in the distance, but it eventually stopped.

All the animals stopped.

So did Stillborn.

CHAPTER 23

James Lappeus stood on the old stone steps leading to the so-called Witch's Castle. Holding a shovel, he stood with his back to the structure itself, looking out across the property that once belonged to Danford Balch so many years ago. The air was cool now, and thinking back, James couldn't remember a time when it wasn't chilly at the Balch homestead.

The last time he was here was when the Balch family still owned the property. It had changed hands a few times over the years, eventually becoming the property of the city of Portland itself. In the 1930s, this structure was built, serving as a ranger station, but sometime in the 60s or 70s, it fell into disrepair and was now mostly used as a place by high schoolers to skip school, drink, and vandalize the property.

He remembered Balch's wife Mary Jane greeted him the last time he was here. She was eager to see him, hoping he'd brought news of her husband's arrest. And he did, but he also brought her an offer. One-thousand dollars to orchestrate her husband's escape from jail.

She didn't take it well. Not having that kind of money on hand in 1859, she frantically approached friends and family looking for loans. When Mary Jane didn't show up at his office with the money, he had no choice but to let justice run its course.

He didn't even see her at her husband's hanging. Danford's stepdaughter Anna was there, but not his soon-to-be widow.

And he hadn't thought about the Balch family since.

Not until this morning after the events in Kenton.

Realizing there was no real reason for the quest that thing sent him and his Hounds on, James spent as much time as he could spare thinking back to when he last saw Mary Jane Balch. She begged and pleaded with him to release her husband.

But looking back now, it didn't seem to be out of love or even fear. She was angry.

His experiences with Edouard Chambreau introduced him into an unnatural world of dark magic and even darker powers. Locations – like his Oro Fino Theater or even the Goldendale Observatory – could be connected to vast resources of something devilish. He learned that from his friend Chambreau as well.

Before that thing replaced him.

James looked in the direction of the zoo. Stillborn would be well into causing the distraction he needed to keep Solemn Judgment away from what he was doing here. When the thing-that-was-not-Chambreau revealed Balch's name, James knew then what he needed to do. The clock and whatever was in that chest they recovered didn't really matter.

James spun the shovel's handle around in his palm. Buried on this property, not too far from the building itself, was a body.

He would dig it up.

There were rumors about why Balch emptied a shotgun into his new son-in-law's face after he and his stepdaughter eloped. Anna was Mary Jane's daughter from a previous marriage, and the word around Portland's bars, especially after nights Danford drank more than his fill, was that Danford viewed Anna as more than a stepdaughter. Sometimes he called her property.

Sometimes he called her even more than that.

Before the hanging, Edouard Chambreau told James that Anna had a child with Danford, and that it didn't survive.

That was Edouard Chambreau back then, wasn't it?

In the distance, James heard gunfire. He thought he could see flashes of white and green to the south. That was good. That meant Stillborn was doing what she was supposed to do.

James faced the old building.

Its thick stone work was covered in moss and graffiti. As he ascended the steps, he looked up at the archway. In yellow paint, someone had scrawled the word 'Love' on its underside.

From what Chambreau told him, it sounded like Danford thought he loved his stepdaughter. Unsurprisingly, she didn't return the feeling. When Anna ran away with a feuding neighbor's kid to get married, Danford got angry, got drunk, and got his shotgun.

The building that came to be known as the Witch's Castle had fallen into disrepair years ago, but that didn't stop the city of Portland from installing a walking trail to it. Of course, the city never called it the Witch's Castle. If it was labelled on a map or trail sign, they called it the Stone House.

Witch's Castle sounded more exciting to students wanting to find somewhere to throw their Friday night parties, though.

James walked through the structure. He looked up from inside the building. It had no roof, that part of building having collapsed at some point in the 1960s. It looked like at some point the city had tried to clean up the site, but so many layers of paint on the walls told James Portland stopped caring all that much about their Stone House.

It was an overcast day. The shadows cast from the nearby trees were muted. Everything was shades of grey and green. But James thought he saw something dark moving in foliage.

Keeping his eye on where he saw movement, James descended the steps and made his way into the clearing in which the Witch's Castle sat. He stopped at a sign pointing out the direction of Lower Macleay Trail running along Balch Creek.

He waited at the sign, watching, listening, but not sensing anything. He could stand there and wait, but he had work to do.

James unbuttoned his jacket and vest with his free hand. Where would he start digging? The unmarked grave of an unnamed child. That wasn't much to go off of, he knew. It was a large property. Where would Balch have buried the infant?

He reached out with his senses. Feeling his eyes flutter shut, he looked inward, searching for the power given to him by Chambreau. There. In the back corner of his mind was the fire. A tiny flame he could will into something larger.

James' eyes opened. It was still overcast, but now instead of greys and greens, the landscape was brighter. Light yellows and unholy pinks. The graffiti on the Witch's Castle seemed to glow.

He cast his gaze around the clearing, to the large fallen tree and the Lower Macleay Trail sign.

The sharp contrast flickered as he narrowed his eyes. He paced, scanning the area.

And there it was.

A spot on the ground not too far from the Witch's House itself, not radiating bright yellows and greens, but black. It was a dead patch of ground.

James closed his eyes and withdrew the magic back into the recessed of his mind. When he opened them again, the world looked like it had before.

But now, he knew where he had to dig.

He took a few steps in the direction he'd determined to the this unmarked grave, but stopped when he saw it again.

Out of the corner of his eye, James saw movement. Something dark slithered beneath a low-hanging plant, hiding beneath wide leaves, slipping across the ground toward the creek. James had a sudden vision of what he saw at the observatory. Feathers. Bone. Black tendrils.

The shape slid like a patch of dirty oil through the water toward him, and then emerged, standing like a man.

No. A woman.

James lifted the shovel defensively as it oozed across the forest floor, picking up small rocks and fallen leaves. A handful of white spots gleamed where its head would be before forming into the shape a dual-layered smile. Inky black flowed around its obscene mouth shape, settling down its neck and resting on its shoulders and hips.

He took several steps back, but the thing followed James.

Two slits opened above where its nose would be, revealing two bright eyes. The teeth opened and a sloppy voice spilled from its mouth.

"Hello James."

James poked at it with the shovel.

The shovel's blade sunk chunkily into its center mass. Four feather-like shapes flipped out from its back, reached around, and snatched the tool from James' grip.

James turned and ran back to the building.

Rivulets of infested slime ran along the ground and easily passed him on either side. They slid up three of the heavy stone steps, then came together, coalescing into that horrid humanoid shape.

James' shoes kicked up pebbles as he skidded to a stop.

The mass extended its feather shapes again, then snapped them back into its back. The teeth opened again. "Did you find my granddaughter?"

James tried to twist away as it flowed back down the steps to him. At first, he thought his feet could not move, but when he looked down, he saw his shoes had been overtaken by the ooze coming from whatever this thing was.

The black jelly moved up his shoes and over his ankles. All his body heat was sapped away. His calves cramped as his muscles froze.

He squirmed and shifted his weight back and forth, from left to right as it crawled up his thighs and waist. Some of it splattered against his wrists. He pulled against the webbing and yanked himself to the side as hard as he could.

James felt the air leave his lungs when he hit the ground. Something in his shoulder crunched, but he could heal that later. He could still move his arms. That's all that mattered.

He scooted away from the Witch's Castle, kicking hard against the form still trying to slide over his body. James felt the cold leaving his legs the harder he pushed back. If he could only get far enough away, he could open a portal.

James crawled on his back into a shadow. When he looked up, he saw Arturo Banks standing above him.

CHAPTER 24

Art reached down for Father Override, and yanked him to his feet. The bottom half of the man's body was wet with something dark. Art shook him, shaking some of the viscous fluid free, and then shook him again to get his attention.

"Father Override, you're coming with me."

Art heard a woman scream.

"No!"

A rocky tendril of gritty black slime lashed out from the Witch's Castle and hit Art in the stomach. He doubled over, dropping Father Override and losing his breath.

"He's mine! He has to dig up my granddaughter!"

Another tendril swung at Art, catching him in the forehead. Art's head snapped back, and the world went white for the briefest of moments. It reminded him of getting hit on the football field.

As his vision cleared, he could hear Father Override trying to scramble away. Art reached for him, but another arm of slime caught Art's wrist and flowed over his hand. For the first time since his first encounter with Father Override, Art felt cool. Where this thing had attached to him, Art's skin and muscles no longer felt like they'd been burning. He pulled his hand back and held it front of his face. The slime pulsed over his fingers, and revealed it was made up of more than just this black ooze. Small stones, something that looked like a tooth, several fingernails, and clumps of hair moved over his hand, and then down his wrist.

Father Override made it to his feet and ran.

The substance covering Art's hand ripped itself from him, and launched at Father Override. It landed on the base of his back, splattering into a thin sheet of muck. Father Override fell face first. The slime webbed itself over him and held him to the ground.

Art flexed his fingers. They were warm again, and seemed to have taken no damage.

Good. That meant he could still make a fist.

"That man is mine!" The shape was walking toward Father Override. The black thick liquid form spread and stretched as it moved. Art tried to look away as bones and gristly muscle rose to its surface. Its shape looked more human with every movement toward Father Override, and eventually more female. At first, it – she – was naked, but from somewhere within its – her – body, clothing sprouted and covered it.

She was now an older woman, wearing a dress that looked like something out of one of those old black-and-white Western shows his grandfather watched. Her tied-back gray hair dripped ink down her front and back. Black liquid gathered in the creases of her tired face. When she opened her mouth to speak, Art thought he saw fur and claws inside her mouth instead of a tongue. Her head rolled in his direction.

"I will have James Lappeus."

"Who?"

"This man." Something dark dripped over her finger as she pointed at the prone Father Override. "He is owed me. You . . . you are another matter."

The arm with which she pointed at Father Override snapped toward Art. Her fingers opened and turned black. Five jets of opaque black liquid launched themselves at his chest.

He tried to turn, but the older woman – if that's what she was – was too fast. Five bolts of cold slammed into his body. Art was pushed back as the chill settled into his body.

Father Override struggled. Facedown, he tried to crawl away, but the dripping black blanket of ooze held him to the ground. "Don't let her take me, Arturo! Please!"

Art shook his head and rubbed his chest. Again, he felt the cold where this woman-thing attacked him. It was so cool, so normal.

"He cannot help you, James."

Was that Father Override's name? Just . . . James?

The bottom of the woman's dress blew back as she leapt onto Father Override's back. The connective webbing holding him down splattered as she pounded into his back with her fists.

Art started for the woman. Her back was to him, and she seemed to be solely focused on Father Override. She brought her hands up, the dark slime formed around them, and she'd pummel the back of Father Override's head and neck. With every moist punch on his body, he'd grunt or groan.

Each grunt or groan was weaker than the previous one.

Art needed Father Override alive. He had to stop this.

The woman hesitated with her next punch. Her hand wavered above her head, and this time instead of the black slime covering her first, the substance hardened. It flashed full of dirt and teeth and muck, and then shone as it formed into a knife.

Art launched himself at her before she could bring it down on Father Override's skull.

With a mighty wet tear, she was torn off the man's back. Inky pools of ooze spread across the forest floor, but those pools moved to puddle around her as she stood.

Father Override reached for him. Art yanked him up by his shoulder and held him protectively to his side.

"You have to protect me, my child."

Art squeezed Father Override's shoulder. "I'm not your child."

"Child?" The woman's jaw dropped low. "Where is the child buried, James?"

Father Override shook his head. "I'm not going to tell you, Mary Jane."

The woman's hands grew into large obsidian blades that then split and then split again and again until all that existed at the ends of her arms were blossoming black blades. They shimmered as she pointed them at Father Override. "Give him t."

He felt Father Override's body stiffen. Art looked at the woman. "No."

She screamed something incomprehensible at him.

If she took Father Override from him, his hope for being returned to normal would be taken as well. He couldn't allow that. Art shoved Father Override to the ground before charging the woman.

She heaved her many-mini-bladed hands in front of her.

Art ducked low and let his horns knock her arms away before lifting her from the ground.

She kept screaming. Her voice seemed to shift from that of an elderly woman to something even older, then to a baby crying, and back to the older woman. "You're ruining everything!"

She slammed her hands into his back. He felt the knives easily dip into his skin. Where they cut him, it was so cold, but only for a moment before his blood erupted and burst into flames. She screamed again, and kicked at him.

Art tried to spin her around to wrap his own arm around her neck like he had with Stillborn, but this woman's skin wis slippery. Some of it even seemed to slide off her body. She wriggled to the ground and oozed up the stairs of the Witch's Castle.

Father Override was on his hands and knees, watching but dancing his fingers over the ground.

The woman's body lost its shape and turned into an undulating mass of dirty black slime.

As flaming blood trickled down Art's back, he reached for a nearby tree. His large hand easily wrapped around it as he tore it from the ground. He threw it at the Witch's Castle stairs.

The thing separated into two halves to let the tree pass through it. The tree snapped against the heavy stonework and rolled away in pieces. The thing came back together into one solid form.

Father Override got to his feet.

Small pools of fire formed behind Art as he approached the Witch's Castle.

An oval-shaped hole formed where the woman's head once was. Three tendrils covered in feathers and scales shot toward Art. He batted the first two away, but grabbed the third one and yanked.

It icily snapped off in his hand.

Art tossed the pieces away.

Father Override returned to his side. "You have to destroy her, Arturo."

"Who is she?" Art didn't look at him.

"It doesn't matter."

"Who's Mary Jane?"

"Someone who should have died years ago."

The thing cried out. "You took everything from me, Lappeus!" The words seemed to bubble out of its center mass. "And I will take everything from you!"

"You can't let that happen to me." Father Override held on to his arm. "If you protect me, I will give you whatever you want."

Art tried to push Father Override behind him again. "Stop talking."

Father Override didn't fight Art and let himself be moved.

"No!" Two more tendrils lashed out at them. Art stood his ground, but felt Father Override slap his back. The open wounds from that thing's previous attack stung. He heard Father Override gasp, and he turned to check on him.

Another tendril – this one ending with a serrated edge – slapped and sawed against Art's thick neck.

Cold flooded Art's body when the knife edge sliced into muscle. Then fire fountained from the wound. His hand went to his neck to control the bleeding. Between his palm and his neck, he caught the tendril. It turned limp being pressed against his neck and the lava-like blood now spurting from his body.

He thought he heard Father Override muttering something behind him, but if he turned to see what he was doing, Art knew he'd spray the man with his blood.

His blood. He pressed hard against his neck and glared at the thing now standing at the top of the Witch's Castle. Art's neck throbbed. Blood streamed and fire licked down his body. The black slick finally pulled its tentacle away, but not before snagging itself on Art's ear and pulling.

Art felt something tear and now more blood poured onto the top of his hand.

The inhuman thing made of ooze and hate flattened itself and then sprung up and away from the building. It kited itself in the air and soared in their direction.

Art ducked, thinking himself to be the thing's target, but its form flapped and soard over him.

And came to land on Father Override.

Art reached for the sheet of slime and yanked it away. Chunks of it slid free and reached out for purchase on the nearby trees and rocks.

The black mass rolled together and bubbled in Art's grasp. A section of it formed into a head and sprouted gray hair. Eyes rolled to its surface and a tongue appeared. It licked away the outline of a mouth. A dirty barnyard smell washed over Art when it spoke.

"Where is he? WHERE IS HE?"

Art looked to where Father Override was, but the man was gone.

"WHERE?"

Gleaming white teeth flopped out of the thing's mouth and grazed the backs of Art's hands. New teeth fell into place.

"HE HAS TO PAY FOR WHAT HE DID TO MY FAMILY! YOU HAVE TO PAY!"

Its eyes rolled back and black before bursting into tiny blades.

Art jerked his head as hard as he could to the side. He felt the cut in his neck open even more. Blood rushed to the surface and showered the writhing thing in his hands. It burst into flame.

And screamed.

He flung it away and watched it burn.

It screamed his name.

He slapped a palm against his neck and tried to stop the fire and blood.

Someone yelled his name.

The thing flattened again into a sheet of black mold. Its edges curled and smoked in the heat.

"Art!"

It was hard to watch the thing burn when his vision refused to focus.

"Over here!"

He fell onto his knees. The world started to dim, and even the fire started to go out.

"Abby! I've got him!"

CHAPTER 25

Twenty-nine hours, forty-seven minutes since the explosion . . .

As he woke, he was aware of his own slow and steady breathing. His breaths rumbled deep in his chest. Something beeped rhythmically at his side. He felt cold spots across his chest and torso.

When Art opened his eyes, light flooded his brain. Everything flashed white and sterile, and then color slowly seeped back into view. He was on his back staring at a tiled ceiling. Art tried to move his arms, but felt resistance at his wrists. It felt like cold metal.

They were handcuffs. And they easily broke when he curled his arms.

The webbed belt around his stomach also snapped when Art sat up.

"Whoa there, big guy."

Now that he was sitting up, Art was able to look around the room. A skinny man in a doctor's jacket stood nearby with a clipboard. The beeping machine to his left was connected to his body with a series of wires and sensors dotting his upper body. Other machines clicked and whirred. A monitor showed a skipping green line he assumed was his heartbeat. He confirmed that assumption when he tore the sensors off his chest and the green line leveled flat.

A TV was mounted in the corner near the ceiling, but its sound was off. It had been turned to a news channel. Art recognized the person on screen as a local reporter, and since someone had turned on the closed captioning, he could read some of what she was saying.

". . . animals at the zoo are being returned to their enclosures after receiving medical treatment. An Oregon Zoo representative states the zoo is working with local law enforcement and the aug-human Varmint, as well as the Professionals from Washington to help with damage and crowd control. Fortunately there were no human casualties, but some . . . "

"You did good, kid."

Art looked away from the television to see Revenant sitting in a chair next to him. The tall, lanky man in the white doctor's jacket

133

looked up from his clipboard. The jacket didn't seem to fit as it hung loose on his body. Art could see he was wearing something that looked like a gymnast's suit underneath.

Revenant stood up and both he and the doctor approached the bed.

"What happened?" Art's mouth and throat felt dry.

Revenant slowly shook his head. "We're going to need you to tell us that. Are you okay?" He gestured at Art's feet.

His ankles were also chained to the bed.

Art nodded.

Revenant clapped his hands together. "Good. Doc, can you unlock the – "

Art lifted his feet. The chains popped apart.

Revenant didn't seem to mind. "Art, this is Dr. Neal. He's the one who stitched you back together."

Dr. Neal smiled at him.

Revenant continued. "He was at the zoo. Voodoo Cowboy called him in. This is his place, actually."

Art looked at the tall Caucasian man. "Your place?"

Dr. Neal's face rubbered into an unnatural but still friendly grin. "No. This is Troy's clinic. He owns the building. I just work here."

Revenant cleared his throat. "Art, this is Dr. Tristan Neal, also known as Slaphappy."

The doctor bowed deeper than his body should have allowed. He came up grinning again. "Nice to meet you."

Art nodded at him. "Slaphappy?"

"That's me. But here I'm Dr. Neal." He held his clipboard to his side before looking back to Revenant. "He should be okay to leave. I'll let Troy know."

"Thanks, Doc."

They both watched the doctor leave. Revenant sat down in the chair and crossed his hands across his chest. "So, what do you remember?"

"From the zoo?"

"And after."

Art let himself lay back down on the bed. He closed his eyes and thought back. The zoo. The animals. The giraffe and birds. And Stillborn.

He didn't bother sitting up. "Stillborn?"

"She's in custody. Abby magicked her up nice and tight." He paused and seemed to choose his next words carefully. "I saw what you did to her."

Art opened his eyes. "I wanted to stop her, Mr. Williams."

"And you did."

"I wanted to do more."

"I know, and I don't blame you."

Art appreciated Revenant giving him a moment before asking his next question.

"What happened afterward?"

"At the Witch's Castle?"

"We found you afterward and brought you here to the Alberta clinic. Abby stopped the bleeding but you were not making much sense."

Art sat up again and swung his legs over the side. He braced himself on the side of the bed. "Father Override was there."

Revenant took another pause. "Did you stop him?"

Art shook his head. "No. Something else did."

Revenant paused. "Something else?"

Art nodded. "I don't know what it was, Mr. Williams. It kind of looked like a person, like someone's abuela, but in an old dress. But it kept changing and growing knives." He caught Revenant's eyes. "I don't know how to explain it, Mr. Williams. Snakes and tentacles. Or eels. Made of oil and ink and I don't know what else. I know that doesn't make any sense."

"It doesn't, but it lines up with what you said before. I'm sure Deacon can help you remember more."

"What if I don't want to?"

"We need to file a report with the SRD."

"What's that?"

"Service Region Director. Solemn Judgment is a registered aug-human team, Art, which means paperwork." He held a hand up. "You don't have to do the paperwork yourself. Deacon will."

"What kinds of things go into this report?"

"Honestly, kid, I've never seen one. Deacon has always handled it. And he's gotten really good at making sure the government gets the absolute minimum of what they need to know."

The two exchanged weak smiles.

Finally, Revenant stood, "You can tell Deacon about it when we get back home."

"Home?"

"Salem. I'll let Abby knew you're up and about, and she'll take us."

"Mr. Williams?"

Revenant leveled his eyes with Art's. "You really need to stop calling me that, kid. It's Hence."

Art tried to nod. "Okay. Hence. But in the field, it's Revenant."

"That's right. You're catching on, kid."

"I don't know if I want to go back to Salem."

Hence had been reaching for the door, but let his hand drop to his side. "What do you want to do?"

Art looked at the television. The news reporter was still at the zoo. Someone with purple skin and black hair was being interviewed. The text on the bottom of the screen identified her as being Skirmish from the Professionals. She was talking about something happening with the elephants and how they were recovering from their injuries.

"I know the people in Kenton didn't survive what Stillborn did. But those animals did."

"Animals are different, Art. And we had help."

"Help?"

"Other aug-humans."

"Do you think they can help me?"

Hence turned back to face him. Art saw the dark worry in his eyes. "I don't know."

Art's shoulders slump.

"But what I do know is that Deacon is going to try to help you. He's helped me. He's still helping me."

"With what?"

"It's a long story I'll tell you sometime. Let's just say when Deacon files his reports, he doesn't always mention me."

"He doesn't?"

"No, and he probably won't mention you too much until we figure out your situation."

"What about my school? My life?"

"That might have to be put on the backburner, Art. Whatever happens, we need to figure out your next steps and go from there."

Art looked back at the TV. There was more footage of heroes containing and corralling possessed animals, or helping zoo employees and guests escape. The station must have gotten their hands on someone's smart phone footage who recorded a man in flashy tassels and cartoony cowboy gear firing a pair of six-shooters at a mob of angry penguins at the Max station underneath the zoo. He noticed the shooter – the screen identified him as Showdown – wasn't actually shooting the penguins, but was using his guns to keep them from jumping to their death on the Max tracks.

"What did you say, kid?" Hence extended a hand to Art.

Art looked back at him and nodded. "Let's go to Salem."

EPILOGUE

Father Override fell through the portal he created using Arturo Banks' flaming blood. His hands burned from smearing his hands through it, but that was a small price to pay to get away from Mary Jane Balch, if that's what that thing really was.

He left before seeing how that conflict resolved, but after seeing Arturo fight, he assumed the not-Chambreau-Balch-thing did not survive. Not with the amount of blood and fire spouting from the young man's open wounds.

Getting to his feet, James gingerly brushed himself off. He ignored the blistering pain from his palms and gazed around the South Dome of the Goldendale Observatory. Apart from himself, the room was empty. It felt bigger than it had before. Some of Stillborn's Born Again were no doubt in other parts of the observatory, but here he was alone.

And those Born Again would be dead at this point anyway.

Before tending to them, though, James ascended the stairs to the telescope. There was no headache beckoning him to it this time. No calling from whatever space that thing resided in when it wasn't here in this room with him.

Arturo must have stopped it.

James didn't bother looking in the eyepiece. Instead, he twisted a gear and adjusted a few dials. Satisfied that the telescope was no longer focused on IC 2118, James returned to the floor and left the South Dome.

There were several bodies, all bleeding from their temples, all still, spread across the floor before him. It would take some time to clean this up, especially now that he was alone. If she was still alive, Stillborn was no doubt taken into custody at this point. Without her and her brother, James set to doing the menial work himself.

Stripping off his jacket and vest, he bent over and slid his hands underneath a dead Born Again's arms. He awkwardly dragged the corpse down the hallway and to the entrway. James opened the front of his shirt and returned to do the same with the next body.

And the next.

And the next.

It took nearly an hour, but at the end of it, a sweaty and winded James Lappeus had moved all the bodies to just outside the observatory itself. There was more than enough blood for him to create a new portal, and since this blood wasn't on fire, it didn't sting nearly as much.

The pit opened several feet away from the entrance doors. He placed it there on purpose as he didn't want to damage the building. Gouts of flame fingered their way from the portal and started consuming the bodies as James rolled them into it. The smell of rotten meat assaulted his senses, but he carried on, disposing of the Born Again.

When finished, he closed the portal and returned to the observatory. The utility room where he had kept the canonic chest earlier was his new destination. Of course, the chest was gone. That slab of oily black mucous had absorbed it earlier when it finally revealed its true form to him.

Unlike that chest they retrieved from Blackstone Hall, what James needed at that moment was still in the utility room.

He wheeled the mop and bucket out. There was a lot of blood to clean up.

James hadn't done this much manual labor in several years. His back and shoulders ached, and sweat soaked his hair and goatee. Finally, after what felt like several more hours, the Goldendale Observatory smelled like cleaning products and was free of blood.

There was one last thing to do. When he returned the mop and bucket to the utility room, he saw it on one of the shelves. A Goldendale Observatory security uniform.

And James thought it might just fit him.

Outside, a bald eagle with a blinding headache and matching seeping wounds on either side of its skull flew north.

DEREK M. KOCH

Coming Late Spring 2023

The Nixon Protocols

Book 1

A 6-Week Rotation Superhero Novel

The once-amnesiac alien turned superhero known simply as Rothchild strode into the conference room prepared for him and his team by the local Service Region Liaison. He made a point of meeting the eyes of the Federal agents already assembled here waiting to hear from the country's permanently-assigned superhero team. Even though he had been on Earth for over twenty years, an active superhero for just over fifteen years, and a member of the Nixon Protocols team for just over three years, Rothchild knew that, in the end, he was a being from another world. As far as he knew, he was the only one of his kind on Earth, and despite his position as the Field Leader of the Nixon Protocols team, his being "not from around here" still made some people nervous. He made himself wear a friendly smile whenever he walked into a room of people he had just met.

But he didn't smile too broadly. What he and his team were here to discuss was not something worth smiling about. Cold Boy was already sitting with his feet and his tablet on the table. He nodded back at Rothchild when they made eye contact. The third member of their field team – Jaywalk – would join them after he finished recovering from the teleportation that brought the three of them to Vancouver, Washington. The man was no doubt in the break room downing his third sports drink at this point.

He wasn't needed at this point anyway, and his vibrating form could be off-putting to those who didn't know what Jaywalk did or how his powers worked.

Ronnique Marroquin, the assigned FBI liaison, cleared her throat as Rothchild approached the front of the room. She didn't need to. The dozen or so agents in the room were already quietly waiting for Rothchild to begin. If anyone needed to be brought to attention, it was Cold Boy, but he only grabbed his tablet.

Cold Boy's way of diffusing any tension from having multiple superpowered individuals in a room of non-Augmented humans at the same time was to appear borderline disrespectful and all-too-lazily-normal. Letting anyone dwell on the fact that he could draw the heat from a man's body in less than a second, or bring a room's temperature to absolute zero in just a few seconds longer would not make a crowd like this comfortable.

And it usually worked. Rothchild, on the other hand, didn't have that luxury. He couldn't blend in. He couldn't just sit around in a room and hope no one paid attention to him. The right half his body and face was an unnaturally dark gold color. Otherwise, he appeared human if not for that golden division running perfectly down his body. During his first few years on Earth, he tried to hide behind make-up and foundation, but using his powers – flight, the cosmic energy blasts he could generate from his fists, his ability to take more than a few punches – usually led to his make-up being smeared away. During his time with the Professionals in Seattle, he finally gave up on hiding his alien heritage, and revealed his origin to the world. His time as a Professional in Seattle and the good that he'd been doing helped to lessen the legal ramifications that came from hiding his true identity. That he somehow became field leader of the country's official superhero team still surprised him.

His appearance still made for quite a sight for those not familiar with him. For that reason, he was always positioned face front and forward at press conferences, in interviews, at recruitment events, and academy graduations. Getting the public used to his being an alien was part of his job.

Today, though, his job was to find out who was killing the supervillains.

He waited until Cold Boy finally looked up from his tablet and made eye contact. They exchanged a brief nod, and then Rothchild began.

"Thank you, Agent Marroquin, for having us." Rothchild paused for Agent Marroquin to tilt her head in acknowledgement before continuing. "It goes without saying, but I'm going to say it anyway, we're all on the same team. We're not here to take over your investigations. This is your case."

Learn more about the 6-Week Rotation series of superhero novels at
www.6weekrotation.com

About Derek M. Koch

85% writer. 85% gamer. 70% podcaster. 95% podcaster. 65% YouTuber. 40% Twitch streamer. 100% bad at percentages. Derek M. Koch is the creator of the 6-Week Rotation (6weekrotation.com) series of superhero novels as well as the **Supernatural Solutions: The Marc Temple Casefiles** series. He is also the designer behind the RPG supplement **Harsch Tables, Volume 1**.

If you can't find him at Monster Kid Writer (monsterkidwriter.com), you can find Derek producing the Rondo Hatton Classic Horror Award-winning **Monster Kid Radio**, the weekly podcast devoted to the classic, and sometimes not-so-classic, monster movies of yesteryear; or you can find him on Monster Kid Radio's YouTube channel or Twitch stream. He is a member of the Monster Kid Hall of Fame and a recipient of the Monster Bash Life Achievement Award.

When not online, you can find Derek at home in the Pacific Northwest either serving his cat Wednesday, playing with his funny-shaped dice, watching a movie from his collection of monster movies, planning his upcoming wedding to his fiancée Beth, or trying to figure out how numbers work.

Made in the USA
Middletown, DE
11 February 2023

24605501R00086